Val Cornish

welcome to
PURGATORY

Published by

MELROSE BOOKS

An Imprint of Melrose Press Limited
St Thomas Place, Ely
Cambridgeshire
CB7 4GG, UK
www.melrosebooks.com

FIRST EDITION

Copyright © Val Cornish 2006

The Author asserts her moral right to
be identified as the author of this work

Cover designed by Catherine McIntyre

ISBN 1 905226 95 0

Printed and bound in Great Britain by:
CPI Antony Rowe, Bumpers Farm,
Chippenham, Wiltshire, SN14 6LH, UK

Major Players

In 'Heaven':
Adam ('Dam') – Younger brother of Luc and Jayce, later Lord of Upper Domain.
Gaia – First Lady of the Upper Domain (Heaven) – mother of Luc(ifero), Jayce (Jason Christopher) and Adam.
Jason Christopher ('Jayce') – Luc's twin.
Pagan – Half-Sidhe sister of above.
Matthias – Father of Luc, Jayce, Adam and Pagan.

Gabriel ('Gabe') – Gaia's Enforcers – also in Luc's band, The Fallen.
Michael ('Mike') – Gaia's Enforcers – also in Luc's band, The Fallen.
Peter ('Pete') – Gaia's Enforcers – also in Luc's band, The Fallen.
Paul – Gaia's Enforcers – also in Luc's band, The Fallen.

Raphael ('Rafe') – Secretary/receptionist.
Samael ('Sammy') – Head of 'Dirty Tricks Dept'.

In The Inferno:
Lucifero diAngelus ('Lucifer/Luc') – Lord of Lower Domain (Hell) and Purgatory.
Ricky (Enrique) – Barman.
Hel – Mother of Luc's son Joshua.
Ashe – Vampire – Mother of Luc's daughter Trinity.
Phoenix – Mother of Luc's firstborn, Lucas – formerly in Gaia's employ.
Medea – One of Luc's dancers: 'Hell's Angels'.
Cass – One of Luc's dancers: 'Hell's Angels'.
Chase – One of Luc's dancers: 'Hell's Angels'.
Morgan – One of Luc's dancers: 'Hell's Angels'.

Salome ('Sal') – Luc's computer in The Inferno.
Spike – Luc's Soul-Sifter and Enforcer, owner of Elvis, the Hellhound.
Judas ('Jude') – Enforcer.

In 'Hell':
Azriel – Computer wizard.
Herod ('Rod') – Research Dept. Head, later Portal Master.
Infinity – Hell's soul-sifting computer.
Jezebel ('Jez') – Luc's secretary/reception/PA.
Loki – Swordmaster/PA.

Luc's 'Little Devils':
Harri, Kazz, Sheba, Lucia, Marcus, Lee, Paris, Donny.

Other Players:
ElisandeSilvan*ap*Melisande*ad*Sebastine-belCanto-Reya – Sidhe (Faerie) Queen.
Gethin*ap*Silvan*ad*Varesh-belCanto-Rel ('Gethin') – Sidhe Prince.
Shiloh – Lucas's Shaman lover.
Laz – Assassin
Mordecai ('Kai') – Assassin

Welcome to Purgatory
Welcome to The Game

It's always a busy night when The Fallen are playing a live gig. You could say that people move *heaven and earth* to get a good seat. There's Mike on drums, and of course Gabriel on horn. My name is Luc – I tend bar. It's a hard job, but I like it. We don't get much trouble. The occasional drunk picking a fight . . . but only once or there's *hell to pay*. It doesn't do to get me angry. You could say I have the *devil* of a temper.

Welcome to Purgatory.
Welcome, indeed, to
'THE INFERNO'.
The hottest night spot this side of Heaven.
The 'coolest' place in town.

The Fallen had finished their number and ambled over to their 'reserved' booth when she made her entrance. I don't mean came in; SHE never just 'came in'. She always 'made an entrance'.

I began pouring drinks for the gang – Mike, Gabe, Peter and Paul, knowing she was expecting a reaction from me as she glided across the room, gawping mouths on either side as a path parted like the Red Sea.

She poured herself onto a bar stool and leaned across towards me. "Pour one for me when you're through," she said huskily. "You know what I like."

Oh yes, I knew what she liked. So did half the Trojan army, if you'll excuse me telling tales out of school. "Long time no see, Hel. Or is it Eve?"

She looked at me sourly. "Not holding a grudge are we, darling? I apologised for that little misunderstanding."

I rolled my eyes. Only Hel could call the fiasco of the apple 'a little misunderstanding'.

"So how was I supposed to know she was allergic to fruit?"

I smiled. "One Poison Apple, stirred not shaken." I gestured towards the booth. "Just be a moment."

I took the tray across. "Sorry about the wait, guys."

"No problem," Gabe grinned. "We understand – don't we, boys?"

I ignored their comments, rolling my eyes as I returned to the protection of my bar. You'd think that after a couple of millennia they'd grow up, wouldn't you? Yeah, right!

I made a show of wiping the bar. "Can I get you a refill?"

She looked up slowly. "Yeah, why not? I've nothing better to do."

"That I don't believe," I laughed as I fixed another Poison Apple. In the quiet that followed, I realised I'd made a bad mistake. She hadn't been joking. "Hey, no long faces allowed – by order of the management."

A flicker of a smile, nothing more. "I'd better try a smile, then," she said softly.

Oh – hell. She wasn't going to – not Hel! I handed her a dry cloth.

"You're becoming a cliché, Lu," Hel said. "Or I am. Telling my secrets to the barman."

"Well, I can give you absolution and a couple of Hail Mary's if it helps," I offered, pouring myself a drink. If Gabe starts playing the blues, I thought, we'll be calling the coastguard.

To my surprise, Peter (or was it Paul? I never could tell them apart), began to strum on his guitar.

"Go on – you know you want to." Hel gestured towards the dance floor. "Anyone comes, I'll take care of them."

"Well . . ." Ah hell, why not? It wasn't as if they were beating down the doors . . .

[Hi, I'm Hel. Thought I'd take a moment to introduce myself. That's why I asked the boys to play something I knew he could not resist – and Luc does so like to dance. Actually, that's how we met. A salsa marathon. I was there with some revolutionary or other – and there HE was. Tall, dark and handsome, long hair, cheekbones to die for, and talk about a six-pack! Out of ten, we're talking a twelve, baby. Oh yeah!

Well, I just knew I had to dance with that guy. Let's just say we set the dance floor – and the sheets – alight. Literally. That was when I found out just whom I was dealing with. Well, me and the entire New Orleans Fire Department, who had to turn off the sprinkler system afterwards. Talk about a red-hot lover, ha ha!*

Didn't last, of course. No one's permanent with Luc. Not that he's cold – anything but . . . but when your heart is as big as his is you learn to guard it. That's part of the reason why the Big Split with you-know-who happened. Not because Luc didn't care, but because he cared too much.

*Enough of that. Luc's taking off his shirt, and I want to drool. (Not a pretty sight – me, that is.) Luc . . . well, that's where **YOUR** imagination comes in. I won't pry into your fantasies if you don't pry into mine.]*

"So, what's the problem?" I asked, returning to the bar and pouring myself a drink.

She gave me a smile – a genuine one this time. "Getting less important by the minute," she replied. "Must be the ambience – or the company."

"Must be," I replied, pouring her a drink. "The guys are up for a spot soon – why don't you do a number?"

"Any requests?" she asked.

"Whatever turns you on, honey," I said, wondering if I was going to regret it. Three Poison Apples, and . . .

The first number was 'Fever'. Let's just say that if anyone could have any male out of puberty panting for more, Hel could! One thing led to another, and I found myself on the dance floor again, wondering vaguely where the hell I'd left my shirt. (To hide the blood stains; her nails were razor sharp.)

Now, I'm not sure what the guys were playing at – I'm not sure I want to know . . . but that kind of music is enough to heat anyone's blood, let alone mine – and we don't have **that** kind of licence! By the time I peeled her off me, I really *DID* need a cold shower.

That's when HE arrived. Standing there in the entrance, dressed from head to foot in white leather. Few men could carry it off, but HE could.

I left the dance floor, slicking back my hair. HE looked as cool as a cucumber; I was barefoot, bare-chested and dripping sweat. Par for the course, I guess.

"Adam," I nodded.

"Hello, Luc. Long time no see."

"Is this official? Am I being raided?"

A faint smile touched his lips. "If that X-rated performance had gone much further it might have been. Are you going to offer an old friend a drink?"

True – before Dam had become a law enforcer on the side of the angels, we had been friends. The best of friends.

"Sure – what'll it be?"

"Don't tell me you've forgotten," he chided.

"A good barman never forgets a regular," I responded, meeting his eyes. "One Jack Daniels on the rocks."

Adam raised it to his lips and smiled. "I need a word – in private."

There was something about his voice that made me look up. It was going to be one of those nights, I could tell – but we had a history, Dam and I. I guess I owed him. Not least because during one 'operation' I had masterminded a certain young woman had fed an apple to another young woman on my orders. One of whom Dam had been quite fond – or a fond as one of our kind can get about one of yours. One who had been terminally allergic to fruit. (*You won't find that little detail in a certain Book.*)

I looked at him for a moment. Adam hadn't changed much since the last time I had seen him. His blond hair was still short, his eyes still the same – almost as green as my own. A few more lines, perhaps. But there was something *about* his eyes. Something behind them, rather, that tugged at my conscience.

"Okay. Give me five minutes – I'll get one of the guys to take over."

His shoulders slumped slightly in relief. "Thanks, Lucifero."

I hesitated. He was one of the few who could call me that and get away with it. Our eyes met, and I knew he remembered that. That, and other things. I grinned. "Okay, five minutes then I'm all yours."

"I wish!" he laughed. In relief, I wondered? I nodded once and slipped out from behind the bar. I whispered in the ears of the boy clearing the tables and he nodded. As soon as he finished collecting, he would step behind the bar, and I would take Dam into my office.

I wondered what had brought him to my door.

I led the way to my office (Rennie Mackintosh-style, for those who might be interested . . . goes well with my black leather trousers!) – gestured to him to take a seat while I went for a towel to dry myself off, and to find a t-shirt. The first one to hand proclaimed 'I'm too sexy for my (t)-shirt' – but beggars can't be choosers. I poured us both a drink, sat in my chair and put my feet up on my desk. Casual. Apart from the fact that he was in white, I was in black, and we both coordinated perfectly with the decor, I couldn't think of a thing to say. Cool, huh?

"So, what can I do for you?"

"I need a favour. I need you to look after something for me. A package. No questions."

"I – see." I sipped my drink. "Why me?"

"Because I can trust you. Because if you give me your word you will protect it and not pry into it, you'll keep your word."

"There goes my reputation," I laughed, for want of something to say.

"Yeah, well." He gave a half-crooked smile. "It's important, Luc. I **will** tell you there's a risk. A lot of people want it. Are prepared to go to any ends to get it – and I do mean any. I wouldn't ask if I had a choice . . ." If he looked at me with those eyes of his, I thought, I'd find myself saying . . .

". . . Sure – if it means so much to you. Just one question – is it, in itself, a danger to me and mine?"

"No. I promise you that."

"For how long do I need to keep this package safe?"

"I don't know . . . but not long. It should not be for long. After a certain date, it will not matter. I hope. I'm not sure. That's why. If I was sure I would tell you. I'm trying to find out. When I do know – I'm babbling, aren't I?"

"Just a little." I smiled. "Can I – offer you another drink?"

"No. I'd – best be going. I saw Helen downstairs, and you know how jealous she gets."

I winced. Too close a memory for comfort that one, even after all these years. "You have a point. Still –" I rose slowly and he did the same, finishing the drink in one gulp and setting the glass down gently.

"Another time, perhaps."

"And – the package?"

"Will arrive by courier. As soon as I can arrange it." He raised a hand to touch me lightly on the cheek. "Thanks, bro. I'll owe you."

A few moments after he had gone, Hel walked in.

"Hey."

"Hey yourself," I replied, glancing her way.

"Trouble?"

"Hope not. Just – a favour."

"Okay. I won't pry." She came across to me. That would be a

first, I thought. "Thought you might want company." Her eyes flickered towards the bedroom.

Now, I (we) don't actually *need* sleep – though it's a useful tool at times for regeneration purposes. She was referring, I knew, to the old horizontal salsa. Whatever had brought her to my door, it looked like I was her choice as elected problem solver too. It was, it seemed to me, one of those nights . . . and who was I to resist temptation?

"Sure, why not? You know the way."

She flashed me a smile and tossed her mane of red hair. "I'll be waiting."

The vision of a red-haired temptress sprawled out on the bed was enough to set my hormones racing. I followed her through the large black doors a moment later. Sure enough, there she was. Laid out on my black satin sheets. I hoped we wouldn't need the fire brigade. I'd just had the place redecorated in red and black, and after my office it's a bit of a shock. A bit of indulgence, you might say. That, and a little tongue-in-cheek poke at my reputation. Give people a little of what they expect, and they don't pry too closely beyond the facade.

It's just a matter of chemistry, I told myself as I shut the doors behind me. Something about the two of us that was purely a matter of chemicals. Still, if it was only a matter of a few singed sheets, I thought, as I removed my t-shirt . . .

I needed a shower, I thought, but Hel didn't seem to care. Later, I knew, I would **definitely** need one.

If we didn't set the sprinklers off, of course.

[Ladies, let me tell you that the sight of Luc walking naked to the shower is something to behold. For myself, I was content to lounge in his vast bed (singed sheets and all). Okay, I'll admit it. The strategic placing of mirrors meant I could savour every delicious moment – and believe me, I did! Whatever else I may be, I'm not a fool!

Did Luc know I was watching? You bet your ass he did. He's not a fool either.]

The phone rang some time later, and Hel answered it before I had time to slip a towel about my waist. I heard her say "Purgatory 666" as I came into the room. She handed me the phone.

"Yeah? Okay. Hold it for me. Better still, put it in my office – I'll unlock the doors. I need to dress."

As I put the phone down, Hel, spare towel in hand, stood ready to dry me off. Another time, I might have been tempted . . . but I simply took the towel, roughly dried my hair and went to hunt for some clothes. Tying back my damp hair, I went to study the package in my office. It was bigger than I had thought. It would need a good hiding place. I had a good place in mind. The problem was Hel. How much could I trust her? And even if I could, should I? After all, a guy needs **some** secrets in his life.

In the meantime, I had work to do. After all, I did not only have a bar to run. That was a sideline. Neutral territory, so to speak. A halfway house between one place and another. Both sides had a say there, even if The Inferno was mine. I had another business to run – and a **VERY** good staff. But I still had papers to sign, etc., etc. After all, one has to pay the bills somehow – true?

"Going to work, honey," I called, as I headed for the elevator.

"Okay," I heard, as I pressed *DOWN*.

As I emerged Jezebel, my secretary, rose to greet me. "Hi, boss. How's things upstairs?"

"Ticking over," I replied. "Any messages?"

"Nothing pressing. Azriel's fried his computer again."

"That's nothing new. His – fourth?"

"Fifth, I think. Ah, Herod wants a new alarm system fitting – something about imps rifling though his underwear . . . Oh, and would you give Peter a call?"

"Did he say what about?"

"No . . . probably admissions, though. A few problems with the Infinity computer – one or two getting through that shouldn't have or something."

"Okay." I went through into my office. The Infinity computer, as you might have gathered, is a soul sifter. When you're sent before it, it decides whether you go up, down, or to Purgatory while you're sorted. Once in a while, like all computers, it (or she, as she prefers) screws up. Some things never change, right?

I shuffled papers, figuratively speaking, for a while. Then called Jezebel. "Jez . . ."

"Boss?"

"I'm going to do a little tour. Have the boys fire up the Harley, will you?"

I heard her laugh. "Sure, boss. Itchy feet already?"

"You know it, babe."

"I'll get right on it."

One of the perks of the job is choosing your own transport, I thought. In the old days, it had been the Hellsteed . . . but although I still had one, I didn't ride him often. I preferred my motorcycle . . . or one of my other vehicles. (What I used depended on my mood. If I was in a good mood, it would probably be the Harley. If I wanted to impress the ladies, it might be the Lamborghini [Diablo, of course, sic!], and if I wanted to come on strong, I have a mean mother of a black Hummer with flames on it.)

By the time I returned to Purgatory and The Inferno, I had blown a few cobwebs out of my system, figuratively speaking. I felt a little better. I don't settle anywhere for long. One or two of the girls were rehearsing on the dance floor – a couple were trying not to tie themselves in knots around the poles. I grinned at Ricky, washing glasses behind the bar, and perched on a stool.

"What can I get you, boss?" he asked.

"Surprise me."

He grinned. Ricky was nothing if not inventive. He was my usual choice behind the bar when I was not there – and a demon when it came to inventing new drinks. I watched him work with the admiration I usually reserve for an artist.

"Try this one."

I sipped cautiously. It tasted good. When I took a longer drink, however, I felt it right the way to my toes. "What the . . .!" I choked. "What's in that?"

"Boss, you don't want to know!" he laughed, and then peered at me uneasily. "Er – don't you like it?"

"It's – incredible!" I laughed. Hell's bells, I could STILL feel it coursing through my veins. A couple of those, and **I'd** be the one dancing half-naked on the tables. (Come to think of it, I often did.) "What's it called?" I sipped cautiously.

"I rather thought you might like to name this one," he offered shyly.

I grinned at him. "How about 'Temptation'?"

He nodded. "'Temptation' it is, boss."

I rose to my feet, shaking myself to clear my head. I'm not usually affecting by drink – none of us are, unless we want to be (unless one is predisposed to be), but this one – I had a feeling Ricky was right. I didn't want to know what was in it.

Still, it might be useful if I wanted to let my inhibitions go. Or it might be a useful weapon, if a little blackmail material would be useful.

I was in my office above The Inferno when my emergency beeper went off.

"Yes, Ricky. What's the problem?"

"Crowd just come in, boss. Newcomers. Smells wrong."

"Okay." I trusted Ricky's instincts and put on the viewers. Something told me trouble was brewing. That it was a set-up. A testing of the waters, so to speak. It was too early for the usual kind of trouble.

I made a point of putting on my reinforced boots, my body-armoured jacket and tied back my hair. If it came to a fight (and it would!), I did not want to be blinded by my hair. My jewellery, also, was chosen with care. Artful, yet guaranteed to cause the maximum amount of damage. Then I went downstairs.

As I entered, I lit a cigarette (don't try this at home, folks – I'm past the stage where it can damage my health), and seated myself strategically on a stool with a view of the floor. Ricky came over to me, leant towards me.

"Got 'em, boss?"

"Oh yeah." I was watching them, alright . . . and if they laid one finger on one of my girls . . . "I think a little 'Temptation' might be useful."

"Coming up, boss."

I'd forgotten how potent a drink it was. Or did not expect the effect on my adrenalin-heated blood. Or perhaps it was my metabolism. All I know is that I was across the room in a fluid motion that impressed even me.

"I'd be obliged if you did not handle the girls, gentlemen," I said softly. "Or I'll have to ask you to leave."

"You and whose army?" one of the newcomers asked.

As I lifted him off the floor with one hand, my rings pressed in a very sensitive spot, I smiled. "I don't **need** an army," I said, launching him across the room with a flick of my wrist. To say pandemonium broke out would be an understatement. Fists were flying, as were feet, bodies and furniture. It was over quickly. My staff are no slouches when it comes to emptying out the trash, so to speak.

"I'll arrange for the refuse to be collected," said Ricky, handing me a cloth for my split lip.

"Get some ice on that eye," I instructed, casting an eye about the room. I was satisfied.

Sitting down, I caught a glimpse of my reflection. I looked a little dishevelled, so I tidied my hair and straightened my clothing. My eyes, I noted, were still glowing. They have a habit of doing that at times like this. (I'm told – reliably – that they do it at other times too. Hel tells me that the first time she saw them glowing at her in the dark . . . well, in other circumstances it would have given her a heart attack.)

"Whoa, honey." I came back to reality and smiled at Hel's reflection. "Did I miss anything interesting?"

"Not much," I replied.

Her hands slipped down the front of my shirt. "Something tells me different. I like to watch you work, Luc. You're so delightfully – ruthless." I pulled away from her sharply. "Ooh, did I hurt your feelings?" She laughed harshly – not a sound I liked.

What was wrong with her? The only time that Hel acted this way was when she was jealous . . . and there was no one around for her to be jealous of. That I knew of. At least, no one whom Hel would consider a rival. No one who would cause Hel to drape herself around me like a boa constrictor.

Only when I saw Ricky's face split into a broad grin, a sideways glance at Hel's expense, did I turn my head. When I saw the tall, willowy figure making her way across the floor towards me, *then* I understood.

I separated myself from Hel and rose slowly to my feet. My heart was thumping. I called myself a fool.

A mischievous pair of eyes met mine, almost at equal height. She was one of the few people around almost as tall as I.

"Well, hello."

"Hello, Phoenix. What brings you downstairs?" I asked, hoping I sounded casual.

"Just paying a social call. Hel."

"Nice to see you again, Phoenix," Hel said, a blatant lie if ever I heard one.

"Can I offer you a drink?" I asked. "Or are you on duty?"

Phoenix laughed. "It's allowed."

"How is she, by the way?"

"Just fine. Gaia sends her regards."

I bet she does, I thought, as I watched Ricky set them up. I really ought to get to work, but I was a little uneasy. The last thing I needed was a catfight. Not that it would do my reputation any harm, I thought. Hel's temper seemed to be matched by the fire of her hair as she sat on one side of me, smouldering.

Phoenix, calmly sitting on my other side, appeared unconcerned. I had an enticing vision of both of them decorating my bed. Danger, my conscience warned. Thin ice! However, the fact that Phoenix worked for HER, the Lady upstairs, had seldom concerned me before. I sipped my drink in the hope it might clear my head.

"Care to dance?" I asked, extending a hand. There I go, I thought, letting my mouth take over. I ought to know better. Don't mix business with pleasure. Don't – oh what the hell . . .!

"Why not?" replied Phoenix, slipping to her feet. I saw Ricky nod across the room and the music changed. Oh, you wicked boy, I thought. Ricky knew only too well what Hel's reaction would be. (Do I need to tell you that he doesn't really like her?) He also knew the state of my bloodstream. I suppose I could have suppressed it, but at that moment I didn't give a damn. The only thought that crossed my mind was that if Dam turned up, we really *would* get arrested. Mind you, so would half my clientele, who were equally enthusiastic about the Latin beat.

Sooner or later, I would have to ask her why she had actually come, after so long. For the moment, I was happy to have her body pressed against me and have my hormones play kiss chase.

"So, why *are* you here?" I asked, some time later.

Phoenix untangled herself from her hair and smiled. "Nice line in pillow talk you have."

I chuckled. (Okay, so we ended up in the sack – what did you expect?) "Sorry. I'll try harder."

She laughed throatily. "Yeah, I'll bet." Half laid across me, her hair tickled. (She can sit on her hair, and she's almost as tall as me . . . do you *really* need things spelling out?)

"Seriously."

She sighed and pouted. "Your presence is officially requested upstairs."

Of course . . . and I bet I knew what about. "Okay. I'd best make myself presentable."

"Now?" she asked.

I laughed. "I'd rather get it over with. You know how much I like it upstairs."

She sighed, "Go for it, then," and settled herself back in my bed. Phoenix is one of the few women who take less time to dress than I do. I dressed with care. Showmanship was the key. It was EXPECTED. So, black leather boots (silver tooled, silver toecaps); leather pants (black, of course, tight); shirt (white, close fitting); leather coat (black, calf length); jewellery – silver rings (lots). That should do it, I thought, tidying my hair. Loose, I thought. Strategic use of makeup (not too much) – this was, after all, very much a performance on her side as well as mine. A state visit, you might say . . . from the head of one to another.

If she wanted the prodigal son to return, however, Gaia was going to be very disappointed. I liked my life just fine. Return to the discipline upstairs? Yeah, right!

As we rode the elevator upwards, I slowly undid a couple more buttons on my shirt, casting a sideways glance at Phoenix. She rolled her eyes and bit her lip to suppress a laugh.

Just enough, I thought. Just enough to show the head and upper part of the snake tattoo which wound its way from my heart (head), around my body, tail pointing downwards from below my navel. Gaia hated it (which was partly why I had had it done in the first place, of course). A little childish, perhaps, but I had felt entitled at the time. I was telling myself not to play it too strong. Arrogance could look like petulance, if mishandled. I would be calm, I told myself. She could not intimidate me anymore, as she had when I was younger. I was master of my own life, my own Domain. Not subject to her rule. The day I had walked out of her door, I had closed it very firmly behind me.

As we stepped out, the cold ice-white decor chilled my blood. I straightened myself and walked towards the secretary's desk, Phoenix forgotten at my side. "I'm expected," I said.

"That you are, Luc. Go right on in."

"Good to see you again, Raphael. Long time no see."

He smiled. "Too long. I'll see you when you come out."

I nodded and walked towards the doors. They opened with a fanfare. Subtle, Gaia, I thought. "Good morning, Gaia. You wanted to see me?" I said, as I crossed her room and sat myself, uninvited, in the chair facing her.

"I expected you sooner, my son."

"Well, I had business to attend to," I replied quietly. "You know how it is."

"Oh yes, I know." She looked directly at me, then, "I've missed you."

"Sure you have, Gaia," I chuckled. "It's probably been a little quieter, anyway."

"That it has," she admitted with a smiled. "You used to call me something else."

"I've called you a lot of things over the years," I replied pointedly. I knew what she wanted me to call her, but I was damned if I would. (I was probably damned anyway, by her lights, come to think of it!) "But then, you have called me a lot of things too. What can I do for you?"

"Hand it over, of course."

"Hand what over?" I asked.

"Don't play the innocent, Lucifer. It does not become you."

"I doubt I could play innocent if I tried," I shrugged.

"The package. I want it."

"Package?"

Gaia snorted. "I know you have it."

"I have lots of packages. Be more specific."

"The Ark, then. The Ark of the Covenant and the Holy Grail. Is that specific enough for you?"

"Quite specific, thank you. I'd love to help, honest. But no can do. Sorry, and all that."

"It belongs to us."

"Well, possession is nine tenths of the law . . . and as you don't have it . . ."

"But you do!"

"I never said that. And why should I hand it over, if I do?" I spread my hands. "Now, is there anything else, or can I go back to work?"

"Oh, go crawling back to your pathetic little life!"

I rose slowly. Thank you, Mother, I thought, for making this easier than I had expected. "My life might be pathetic in your lights, Mother dear, but at least I can say I am happy. I have people around me who serve me by choice . . . can you say the same? Go back to your lonely bed, Mother, and ask yourself why Father walked out . . . and if he would have done so if you had been a little more welcoming and a little less . . ." I took a deep breath. I did not want to look into her eyes. Wanted to bite my tongue, before I declared open war between us.

Not since the split had I felt so close to raising hell in those frigid rooms.

Not since I had refused to be her golden boy, her beloved son, her tool.

Not since I had walked out, taking those with me those who would come, and opened the doors that would keep us apart until Hell froze over.

"Enough has been said, Gaia. I would prefer it if we did not meet again. I wish you joy in your life." I turned, then, and walked out without a backward glance.

"Luc –"

I turned at the sound of Raphael's voice. I knew he – and Phoenix – had heard it all. "Be seeing you, Rafe. Take care . . . of yourself, and her."

I owed her that, at least. He swallowed and nodded as, coat flying, I headed for the elevator and pressed DOWN.

I must have looked like hell incarnate as I entered The Inferno – if the bodies fleeing my path were anything to go by! I headed for the bar, where a drink was already waiting for me. A double, I noted.

"Do I look *that* bad?"

Ricky grinned and angled the mirror in my direction. I winced. "Ouch!" My eyes were burning, spitting emerald fire; my hair was wild, my cheekbones taut with anger. What I did NOT need was Hel sidling up to me and attaching herself like a leach. With a snarl, I pushed her away.

"You could have said 'leave me alone'," she said softly. Hurt?

"Leave me alone," I obliged, turning away from her. Ricky placed a pack of cigarettes by my hand. I resisted, but only for so long. Why, I asked myself, had I let HER get to me? The time when her opinion might matter should be long past.

"Thanks," I murmured softly, as another drink appeared. Slowly, I turned to study the club. It was quiet tonight. Hel had retreated into a corner. Wounded. It was probably going to cost me, I thought. Music played softly, and I was tempted to ask for more noise – but the mood I was in was dangerous, I knew. Best keep the profile low. I retreated to my sanctuary, leaving Ricky in charge.

Safer, that, than giving in to temptation and riding my Harley like the proverbial bat out of hell. I **was** tempted, however. Tempted to ride to her gates naked as the day I was born. That would shock a few sensibilities, I thought – but also be incredibly childish. I would not give her the satisfaction.

Instead, I settled down and watched a couple of movies until my mood had improved sufficiently. By the time I had showered and changed I felt considerably improved. I relieved Ricky and looked around to see if Hel was still about.

"She left shortly after you blew through," he said, as a parting shot.

I set about doing the jobs he had not completed. It was too quiet. Too still. I surveyed the faces in the room, looking for 'ringers'. I did not sense any. Yet the feeling of unease remained. Something was going to happen. Soon.

The question was, should I prevent it happening, or should I allow it to happen? There's always something to be said for identifying the opposition. (You know the saying 'better the devil you know'?) There's also something to be said about taking out as many of the opposition as one can!

More to the point, I needed to know what date or time Dam considered important, and what part the 'package' might conceivably play. And why he had chosen **me** to look after it, rather than hide it himself. I was not foolish enough to underestimate his talents for scheming, and for mixing. Almost as good as mine. The question was what he hoped to gain. I suspected he wanted the heat off HIM so that he could do something, by placing it on me. That, and a probable desire to piss Mother off. That was always a temptation, even when you were on her side (Mike, Peter and Paul tell me, anyway). She could get too full of her own importance, but then couldn't we all?

I slipped my com-link out of my pocket, typing a brief request to Research. As I waited for a reply, my senses began to prickle. The hair stood up on the back of my neck. I screamed "**DOWN**!" as the room exploded into flame. Now, this was f***ing annoying, I thought, as I shouted instructions. I spun around, hair and coat flying, as I waited for the sprinklers to kick in. Damn her. Damn her to Hell!!

You're going to pay for this, MOTHER, I thought. Fury turned my blood cold. This was nothing more than a minor inconvenience. The Inferno would not be damaged beyond cosmetic repair. A testing of reaction. Of defences.

I considered my response as I walked towards the door. Should I play tit for tat? Or should I ignore it?

A smile touched my lips as I leaned against the doorframe. I lit a cigarette, inhaled slowly as my senses sought a figure in the mist. Gaia's 'Enforcer'.

"Morning, Arnie," I called. "It's going to be a lovely day. Give my love to Mom." Then I turned back inside. She hated to be called 'Mom' more than anything. Always had.

When I finally got around to checking my com-link, there were a number of references to check. I would need time – and privacy – to go into it thoroughly. Whatever it was, it was sufficiently crucial to drive Adam to ground and Gaia to send in the heavy mob. Still, it was business as usual, and The Fallen were playing.

By the time I made my appearance, the guys were already setting up. Well, all except Mike, who was perched on a bar stool taking to Ricky and eating.

"Nuts," he said.

"Precisely," I responded. "Okay, Ricky?"

"Yeah, boss. No problem."

"I gather you had a little redecorating job to do," said Mike.

"You could call it that." I pulled up a stool. "We had a few visitors who didn't like the decor."

Mike nodded thoughtfully. Now, the guys are neutrals, but their 'boss' IS upstairs after all. "Dirty pool."

"Yeah."

"You want me to hang around awhile?"

I was surprised – and pleased – by the offer. Mike is one of the best fighters I know. Mind you, being Senior Archangel, he was going to be in hot water when Gaia found out. "I'll let you know. Thanks, Mike," I added.

A broad grin lit his face. "No problem. Just say the word." He slipped from his stool and went to do a sound check. At least, that's what I assumed they were doing. Either that or castrating cats.

It was not until I returned down below that I was able to get enough time on the computer to consolidate the bits and pieces I had acquired. I like to keep 'business' and 'pleasure' separate, if you know what I mean. Hence, I don't have direct access to the master computer from The Inferno. Only the usual remote link. 'Salome' thinks I neglect her – and tells me so in no uncertain terms. That was why I half-expected the odd tantrum when I linked on.

"And how may I serve you, O Master?"

I grinned. "Hi, Sal. Sorry for the neglect."

Sniff. *"Is that all the apology I get? You don't call, you don't write . . . then it's 'Hi, Sal!'"*

I did NOT need a computer with PMT! Still, if you had to have a sentient computer, you had to put up with its moods. Part of the package. "I really AM sorry, Sal . . . but I've been busy."

"Yeah, yeah. Okay – what can I do for you?"

"I'm going to input some dates into you. I want you to come up with the most suitable explanation."

Silence for a moment. *"Do I take it you have an idea, and want a confirmation?"*

"Smart girl. Either that, or a better idea."

"Give it to me, boss."

"I like a girl who's eager," I chuckled.

"You just like girls, boss," she retorted. *"But it could be worse, I suppose."* She waited patiently while I inputted the data and a few stray facts which might/might not be useful. If she came up with the same answer I had, I could be in trouble. Particularly as, if I was correct, I could be starting another revolution. *"I have something for you, boss,"* came her response, *"but I don't think you're going to like it."*

That, I thought, was an understatement. "Go on, Salome. Give it to me."

She chuckled. *"Would that I could, boss. Are you sitting comfortably? Or rather, are you sitting?"*

"I am."

"Then here goes. The date you have given me refers to Easter. Monday, to be exact. The Day of Resurrection." A pause. *"That, and the projected closest pass of Halley's Comet since the last one, seventy-six years ago."* 2061. Easter Monday. Resurrection. Rebirth. Oh shit. Shit. Shit!

I had hoped – prayed – that I was wrong. That what I feared was not her intention . . . but I could not see it any other way. There was no other reason I could come up with why she would need the Ark (power source, almost beyond measure if used in certain hands), the Grail (blood/sacrifice) and the Comet (portent of prediction – birth and death . . . 1066 and all that – the birth of a certain child in the stable of a little-known town called Bethlehem). What most people did not know was that there were two babies born that night. One, well, you don't have to be a genius to guess that one. The other – well, naturally that was yours truly. Yup, that's right . . . and another thing that Book doesn't tell you. And Mother intended to reincarnate him on the anniversary of our birthday. (Forget December 25th, folks. That was never right – just no one ever got around to correcting it.)

Jayce had wanted out. He'd wanted to be out of the battle that he knew would come. Mother had always favoured him, wanted him for the 'throne', so to speak . . . but had conveniently ignored the fact that he did not want it, and nor did I. Any conflict between us, any boyhood arguments, had always had Gaia behind them. When he had chosen mortality, Mother had refused to accept it. Had wanted Father to step in, to bring him back. He had refused. Left. She had never forgiven him for that, and for being more human than she had ever been. For having imperfections.

I knew, then, that she had had the Ark secreted away, awaiting the 'right' moment – and that Adam had realised what she intended, and handed me the greatest weapon known to our kind rather than leave it in her hands.

I knew, then, that he believed our mother to be MAD.

Should I bring it out of its hiding place, then? Bring it down here? No, I thought. Not from any philosophical reasons, but because I knew only too well that there were those among my own people who would want to use it as the ultimate weapon to 'take back' upstairs.

That was not my desire, nor my intention. I liked things fine, just the way they were. But without a nut at the wheel, so to speak. I knew, also, that I was going to need a little backup. That when it came down to it, I could not place Michael in jeopardy. Wanted this to be as quiet an affair as possible, with as few casualties as I could manage.

"Thanks, Sal."

"Always a pleasure. That all?"

"That's all. Be seeing you."

"Make it soon."

I sighed, settled back in my chair, steepled my fingers and tapped my lips. "Jez?"

"What can I do for you?"

"Are either Spike or Jude around?"

"I'll find out."

I waited for a moment. Spike and Jude were MY Enforcers. Spike was a little rough around the edges, but good in a fight.

Jude could talk the hind leg off a donkey while kicking ass.

"I have Jude for you."

"Hey, Jude," I said. "Are you busy?"

"Not at the moment . . . nothing that won't keep. Got a job for me?"

"Round up Spike from whatever dive he's in then come to my office above The Inferno. Take the elevator. I don't want you seen."

"Righto, boss. I get it. Will do."

The line went dead, and I sighed. I was going to have to make preparations for war, whether I liked it or not. I did not want to fight, but the folks upstairs might not see it that way.

I returned to my suite, wondering whom I could trust. This was getting too big for me to handle on my own – yet with the stakes being potentially so high . . . Which led me to wonder at Hel's timely reappearance/disappearance. How much could I trust Hel not to sell me out? And Phoenix – we had shared much, but she worked for Gaia. As, in the end, did Mike & Co. If it came down to the wire, how much could I rely on friendship?

If I wanted to keep this quiet, select, what else could I do? There comes a point when you have to – it's called faith. So, I called Mike to my office and lay the 'evidence' before him without actually admitting that I had the merchandise in question. Mike listened, silent, his expression turning to sadness, to pain. "You know how this is going to be written, don't you?"

"Oh sure. Big bad me coercing the good guys into rebellion in order to get back upstairs. If we fail."

"Yeah."

"And if we win . . ."

"We write The Book." Mike grinned briefly and wiggled his eyebrows. "Whatcha goin' to offer, huh?"

"What do you want?" I laughed. "Gold, jewels, girls – peanuts?"

"Ah, my weakness," he replied. "Throw in a few candy bars and I might be interested."

"You got it."

"Okay then," Mike nodded. I wondered how serious he was – or I was. If, under the guise of a joke, I had actually 'bought' the greatest soldier of all time. "You want me to sound out the guys?"

"If you would. It might sound better coming from you."

He nodded. "What other help can we expect?"

"I want to keep it quiet. I'm bringing Spike and Jude up. I'll give the clan here a choice and batten down the hatches."

"Rick will want to play," mused Mike. "He'll be royally pissed off if you don't invite him in."

Michael, Peter, Paul, Gabriel, Judas, Enrique and Spike. My magnificent seven. I could do a lot worse, I thought.

"And we wouldn't want that, would we?" I sighed. "I don't want a war, Mike."

Mike smiled, bittersweet. "I know, Luc. Why do you think I'm still here? Why do you think we're all still here? I know you don't want war. I know you never did. I also know that when it comes to the wall, you don't want the seat upstairs."

Ah Mike, my Michael! You DO know me after all.

[I always did, Luc. One of the hardest things I ever had to do in HER name was kick you out and stay behind. I guess I got complacent somewhere along the line. Too satisfied with the 'status quo' – convinced myself I could fight from the inside . . . but you know and I know what the result will be if she succeeds in bringing him back. If it's done in public – in THEIR world. As it has to be, in the circumstances. The ultimate 'proof', the ultimate truth. GENOCIDE. GLOBAL. One religion against another over proof of Resurrection/Heaven/Hell. The very thing she accused you of wanting to start.

ARMAGEDDON.

Judgement Day.

Whatever.

That's why I'm with you, Lucifer. Because, bad as things are for them, the alternative is so much worse.]

"Do you have any idea where Adam is?" he asked.

"Nope. I suppose Jez could try and trace him – but I'm not sure why he's hiding. Whether it's because he has a part to play in this, or whether it's because he thinks I can handle it better."

"Or if anyone has to take the rap, he'd rather it was you than him," Mike added laconically.

I could not believe my brother was that much of a coward. True, whatever the outcome my reputation would not suffer. If I failed, well, business as usual so to speak. If not – well, that was a whole new ballgame, as you might say. I might find myself as the good guy. Then what would I do?

Any which way, I wanted as few people hurt by this as possible. True, there was unlikely to be any permanent damage, but that was not the point. The point was this was family business. Before anything else, it was family business. It was not a battle on our soil that was the problem. It was only a problem if she got past me and involved your world. That I could not allow.

Forget the religion thing. That is just the excuse. Politics, you might say. What isn't? Call it management, if you like. After all, where do you think I get all my raw material? If she destroyed all life, I'd have more material than I could handle. So would she, but that's not her concern. She can always send them down to Purgatory for a while, while they get sorted. Buy a little time. Conveniently forget that she surrendered any rights over your existence a long time ago, as part of the treaty between us. She wanted to retain control. It was yours truly that fought for your rights to determine you own lives. Sorry if that destroys your illusions. History, as they say, is the ultimate in propaganda, being written by the victors. As far as you are concerned, her side. However, the truth is that SHE wanted to be worshiped, all-powerful, etc., etc. Not me.

"I'll get on it, then," Mike said, sensing that my thoughts were far away.

"Yeah – thanks, Mike. You do that."

I needed a shower – and something to drink. And food. Comfort food. Yes. I needed to indulge myself a little. To plan. To forget, for a moment or two, the reality of what lay hidden beneath my bed. I felt like going downstairs and dancing until I was exhausted enough to sleep. Or drinking myself out of my mind. Anything.

But I was not a fool. I knew it would not go away. That was not the way my mind worked. The truth was, my mind would keep working until it came up with a solution, whether I wanted it to or not. The truth was my natural instincts were to keep going until the end before I crashed out. Then I would sleep the sleep of the just in my big, luxurious, decadent bed alone or not as the fancy took me, and nothing short of – well – Armageddon – was going to disturb me.

Down in the club room, I found Mike and Ricky side by side, moving furniture with the help of some of the girls, most of the clientele having been shipped out with the promise of the bash to end all bashes when this was over. Spike, I discovered, was helping himself at the bar while balancing Jude on his shoulders. Jude was, I **think**, setting up booby-traps. Either that or planning to run away to the circus.

I eyed the lined-up soda siphons with distrust. "Flame throwers," Spike informed me.

"Of course," I nodded. O-kay. "And I suppose those are grenades?" I asked, gesturing towards the fruit, piled high on a platter.

"Sure. You've heard of pineapples haven't you?" Judas enquired. Yes, I did know that it's one of the old names given to hand grenades because of their shape.

"Of course I have," I replied, deadpan. "All we need are splatter guns, the cast of *Bugsy Malone*, and we're set."

"Told you he'd understand," said Spike. "Smart, he is."

"As a razor," nodded Judas.

I sauntered over to join Mike and Ricky, leaving Spike and Jude doing – whatever it was they WERE doing. "Anything I can do?"

"You could reprogramme the music. Something – inspirational."

"What do you have in mind?" I asked.

"How about 'Always Look on the Bright Side'?" Ricky suggested.

"Or 'When the Saints Come Marching In'?"

"Or there's always . . ." I walked away. I was beginning to think my idea about getting plastered was infinitely preferably to listening to those idiots' bad puns, musically speaking.

I settled into a corner and watched them. My people. My friends. Pitching in. For me. For US. The least I could do was come up with a little background music. I could be as crazy as they could, after all. 'Livin' la Vida Loca', might be a good place to start, followed by every bouncy, pulsating tune we could come up with. If it came to the worst, we could always scare them away by playing 'It's a Small World After All . . .'

It was not, as you might imagine, the best time for Hel to walk through the door. Given the fact that I could not trust her, I had little option. If I was wrong, I was adding to my 'account'.

"Ricky, see that Hel is looked after, will you?"

He caught my eye and grinned wolfishly. "Yes, boss."

Hel threw me a furious look as he led her away (to a 'guest

room'). I winced. All I needed now was for Phoenix to turn up.

Phoenix.

While Hel's motives were usually purely financial, Phoenix's were more dangerous. A matter of ideology.

Time was when Phoenix and I had been as close as two people could be. Before the split. Before The Fall. Before a certain Lady had started spreading her poison. I could have had it all: Phoenix at my side; my mother's affection; all the power I wanted – but at a price. A price I had never wanted to pay. I could no more have acted as figurehead, as her mouthpiece, then than I could now.

She had kept Phoenix from me, and then sent her to me one hot, sultry night. Phoenix had told me everything I had wanted to hear. Taught me a lesson I would never forget – and given my mother what she had believed to be the ultimate weapon against me.

My son.

The son I had not seen or acknowledged from that day to this.

Until now, I realised, as my eyes focused on the entrance.

The room fell silent. No surprise.

In a veil of mist stood Phoenix. Her long hair loose, her expression a mixture of pride and regret. Her hand firmly grasping that of a young male child. Slowly, she walked forward and stood before me. Uncertain – even afraid. Of ME? Despite the betrayals, had I ever given her cause to *fear* me?

"Lucas, this is your father. My Lord Lucifer, may I present to you your son?" I looked down at him, then up at her. Her eyes were sad. "Please?"

What the hell do I say, I thought, in the silence? I could feel all eyes on me. Waiting for my reaction. My answer. Oh hell!

"Welcome to Purgatory, Lucas." I offered my hand.

"Thank you, sir." He smiled at me, taking my hand without fear. "Mama tells me you have a Harley. Would you take me for a ride?"

"Er – a little later. I'm a bit busy right now," I mumbled. He did not seem surprised.

"Okay. Hi, Uncle Mike. Can I help you build a bomb?"

I glanced at Phoenix and raised a brow, then at this son of mine. Mike appeared unperturbed. Of course he would know. Everyone knew. Everyone knew Lucas. Except me. But had I not wanted it that way? He smiled. "Sure. You can pass the tools to me." Taking Lucas by the hand, he led him away, leaving a small cocoon of silence.

"Look after him, Luc."

"You're not staying?"

"Not this time. Someone – has to stay and –" She shrugged. I understood.

"But later . . .?"

She smiled and reached up, caressing my cheek. "If there is one, and any justice."

Then she was gone, as suddenly as she had arrived.

I retreated to the bar, poured myself a drink. Spike glanced my way. "He's a good kid, boss. She hasn't got to him." I didn't ask to which 'she' he was referring. Spike had a sense about these things. He was my Soul Sifter, after all.

"Great," I mumbled as I sipped. "Comes recommended by the Grim Reaper and the Terminator."

"Don't be a grouch," he laughed. "You're just pissed off because she caught you by surprise. Think of it another way – you have the weapon now, if it comes to it. Gaia isn't going to like it one bit."

That was the difference, however. I was not going to use him as a weapon. Not when, given her tendencies when annoyed, it might be all of his mother I might ever have. Ah well, I thought. What was one more minor complication? One more to be responsible for? Besides, the kid had every appearance of being able to look after himself. Between Mike & Co., the kid probably knew more than I did about such things.

They seemed to have everything in hand, so after a while I elected to go outside for a smoke. I watched the figures moving about the world outside my door, going about their lives. Acknowledged one or two in passing. I inhaled slowly, watching the shadows. I was unsurprised when a voice at my elbow said, "He's out there."

"Who?"

"Arnie, of course."

"Yes, he is . . . but how do YOU know?"

He grinned. "You can know Uncle Mike and ask me that?"

He had a point. I nodded. "What do you know about me?"

He giggled. "A lot of things you probably wish I didn't." Oh great, I thought. He sobered. "I know what you are, and who you are . . . why you did what you did – not just from Mama, but from others. So it's not just one-sided. I asked to meet you, you know."

"You did? Why?"

"I thought it was about time I decided for myself what to believe."

That was understandable, I thought. "But this is not necessarily the best time."

"Oh, I think it is. After all, how someone handles themselves in a crisis is a measure of who and what they are," he replied.

Don't think of him as a child, I reminded myself. Look beyond the physical. He's your son, and Phoenix's. Brought up by her, by Mike, by Gabe and the rest. He's not **just** a child. I could see myself in him, I thought. He had my eyes – rimmed like mine with gold flecks.

"And if you decided you did not like what you saw?"

"There's always upstairs," he admitted frankly. "But I don't think there's much chance of that. Not the way things are going. Grandma wants me to front for her, you know."

I didn't, but it didn't surprise me. The thought of Gaia being addressed as 'Grandma' . . . Oh but that was almost too good to ignore. "And you don't fancy the idea?"

He snorted. "You've got to be kidding. Not without major restructuring – and redecorating – at least."

I laughed. "I know what you mean. Have they found you a room here yet?"

"No – but I guess they will."

"Or you could choose your own. If you don't like the decor, we can soon change it when this is over."

"I can change things?"

"Sure. I do it all the time."

"Cool!" His eyes shone. "What do you want me to call you, by the way?"

Er . . . "I don't know. What do you want to call me?"

He considered for a few moments. "Would you mind if I called you Luc? I'm not sure – you know – this 'Father' thing is kind of new."

"To both of us. We'll have to muddle through as best we can," I acknowledged. "Sure – call me Luc. I'm happy with that."

"Okay. He's over there, by the way."

I turned my head. "Yes, I know."

"He doesn't look happy."

Arnie never did. But then, given Arnie's expressive range, it was sometimes difficult to be sure.

"Who else is out there?"

He pursed his lips. "Josh, Gideon, Sebastian . . . Max is coming. That's all I can sense. Is that okay?"

"That's more than okay," I replied, and his smile broadened. "Go inside and alert Mike, will you? Ask him to come out here."

"Will do. Anything you want me to do?"

"Check out the rooms, if you like. Unless, of course, you're hungry?"

"Of course I'm hungry," he chuckled. "Mama will tell you I'm always hungry."

"You're a kid – it's allowed," I replied. "Ask one of the girls, they'll point you in the right direction."

"You bet!"

He disappeared inside, and Mike joined me a few moments later.

"The hoards are gathering?"

"Something like that." I offered Mike a cigarette and he shook his head. "Filthy habit," I shrugged. "I'll quit one of these days. Lucas being taken care of?"

Mike grinned. "If he were a little older, I'd be getting jealous. The girls are hovering around him . . ." I smiled. "He's an okay kid, Luc. She's done okay by him. We all made sure of that. Not that Phoenix would have done anything else. Whatever happened between you, she wouldn't have turned him from you. It was – well – Gaia that we were worried about."

"Go on," I said softly.

"Oh, nothing – direct. Just insinuations. Little comments. I'm sure you can guess." I nodded. Oh yes, I could guess. Little comments – right. About how I had 'betrayed' her. Betrayed my twin.

I could remember that day as clearly as if it had been yesterday. How I had gone to the cave to bring him out. Found him there. Talked with him. Heard him plead with me to let him go. He had really believed she would rescue him from the cross, you see. That she would intervene and spirit him away. That would have worked as well as the ascension bit. Been just as good for the public. Better, even. She could have saved him much pain. (Yes, we feel pain. We can be wounded. Oh, we heal – but that does not mean we do not feel pain. We never wanted immunity from pain. It keeps us 'human', if you know what I mean.)

But no, she left him hanging there. I took him water, Mary and I sheltered him from the sun when we could – bathed him . . . When I went to him, he told me, then, of his plans. He was going to be 'resurrected', okay . . . but then he was going to disappear. He knew that Gaia was going to set it up so that we had no choice but to fight. She was going to make that a sure thing – he wasn't sure how. He thought that it was either a) that she knew there were those who were dissatisfied with her rule and wanted to weed them out using me as a focus, or b) that her hold was weakening, and she wanted one sure-fire religious focus. One spectacular, get-'em-all demonstration that she was 'top dog', so to speak.

One way or another, I was going to 'fall', and I'd decided that if that were so, it was going to be on my terms. So, I agreed to help him. I agreed to come back for him, to take him away. Just until the air cleared. Until we could sort things out once and for all.

I still don't KNOW what happened, not for sure. I only know that when I returned, he was dead. That the game played out was one big fake from start to finish . . .

. . . But this time, she was going to do it for real. Somehow, she had found a way to bring him back. What was she going to tell him? That I had poisoned him, and play the whole damned game again, millennia later?

Perhaps he had, as I believed, bribed someone to slip him poison. Perhaps, inadvertently, it had even been me in the drink I had brought him – the only way he could think of to prevent a split that had occurred anyway. "Was it you?" I asked. "Or was it Gabe?"

Mike smiled sadly. "I'm not saying anything, Luc. A promise was made to Jayce – it transcends even friendship."

I nodded. I understood. After all this time, it still mattered – and did not matter at all. "I won't go through it all again, Mike. I won't. If I thought it would help, I'd destroy the damned thing myself."

"Then why don't you?" asked Mike, quietly.

Why? I was damned if I could answer. I could take it downstairs – but that would play into the hands of any of my own people who were plotting 'rebellion' (I was no more immune to that than she was, 'human nature' being human nature). I knew, however, that when I got my hands on my younger brother, I was going to knock seven bells out of him for putting me in this position. No matter what I had inadvertently done to him, he could not expect me to take this lying down.

All I had to do was keep in out of her way until her window of opportunity had passed, and that moment was coming fast. What I had to do was decide what I was going to do then. I would have to hide it, I supposed. Bury it somewhere so far away, so deep, that no one would ever find it again.

I wasn't exactly sure what the Ark could do. I knew what it was SUPPOSED to be able to do. That might not be the same thing. However, it might not matter. If people believed, as in so many things, the reality might not be important.

"I'm damned if I know, Mike . . . but then, as I'm damned anyway . . ." I chuckled. I walked a few steps forwards, raised my hands high. "Come and get it, if you can. Come and get ME. If you can!" Then, in a flash of light and a puff of smoke, I was gone – leaving Mike to follow, coughing, in my wake. He glared at me sourly when he followed me inside. I grinned in apology.

Conscience pricked at me briefly. I knew I ought to go and see Hel. I owed her that at least – but not at that moment. Food was a more tempting prospect. I fancied something to eat. (Eating, like sleeping, is something we don't **have** to do – but some habits die hard, as they say. Besides, it was a useful social activity.)

I need not have worried. As I approached the kitchens, Lucas emerged, followed by a couple of the girls, carrying trays of food.

"Come and get it, boss," Morgan said, calling to Spike and Paul who were crawling around on their hands and knees doing something unspeakable to the drapery.

"Thanks. You still have time to get out of here, girls."

They looked at each other. Chase spoke for both of them. "Don't be stupid, Luc. If we were going, we'd already be gone. Just eat up and shut up." She laughed at my expression. "Call it quid pro quo, if you want. You've looked after us; it's our turn to return the favour. We might not be up to much, but we can patch up any injuries, and carry – stuff."

"Too right," Morgan affirmed. "So just – belt up. Okay?"

I looked at them, defiant, and laughed. I raised my hands in surrender. I knew when I was beaten. Eat, drink and be merry, for tomorrow . . . etc.

It was to no one's advantage, I thought. This whole damned affair. Not even Gaia's, though of course she could not see it. Free will did not only mean choosing to believe in your own destiny, it also meant a right to believe in God – or the Devil – too. Faith – that was the keyword. Not proof. Faith.

I looked at the com-link, counting down to the moment of 'contact'. Whatever I was going to do, it would have to be soon. And whatever SHE was going to do.

One thing I did know was that I had to take the Ark somewhere and bury it deep. Somewhere it would be safe for all time – or at least until it was needed for some rational reason.

Which meant a diversion.

Which meant I had to allow The Inferno to be attacked. So be it.

When I told Mike what I needed, he was not surprised. "For how long?" he asked.

"How long is a piece of string? Until I return. Or signal you to surrender."

Mike met my eyes. "Okay." He extended a hand. I gripped his firmly, briefly. No more to be said.

Let me dress, then, for battle, I thought. Let me dress to face my mother. Let me look into my heart and know the truth that she was wrong – if right or wrong were factors in this game . . . for this IS a game. The Great Game we all play. Perhaps I had been a less than diligent player of late: grown careless. No more.

I felt guilty, leaving my friends to fight even for a while without me – but I was fighting in my own way.

So I dressed with infinite care, and took the Ark once more out of Eternity and back into the world of men. I bore it gently, with the reverence it deserved, to a place of ancient power, a place sacred from time immemorial. The time was as important as the place – my mother is not the only one with a sense of *time*.

As I knelt, waiting, in that sacred ring of stones she came. The Lady. Tall, as fair as the moon, her hair a pale cloud, pale as her robes, pale as death. She stood over me, a hand above my head in blessing.

"What would you, Light Bringer?" she asked in a voice not a voice, echoing in my mind as words because there could be no other way of hearing her. She who came before All, this being, this Guardian. I could trust her to guard this treasure because she, above all, was outside The Game.

"Will you take this and guard it?"

"Why?"

"It should not be a tool in The Game. It is – greater than the game . . . and I do not trust myself to keep it – and not, in some desperate day, use it."

She smiled and caressed my head. "You are wise, my child. It shall be so."

I felt the weight lift from me, and both it and she were gone.

Time for me to return, I thought, and **play**.

I walked into hell, metaphorically speaking. Into the fire. Into and out of the other side. I stood amongst the chaos and confusion, raised my arms high and cried out, "Hear me, Mother. It is over. It is gone." Waited for an answer – a response.

"Gone where?"

I smiled. "Out of here. Out of time. Out of The Game."

"I could have brought him back!"

"Against his will!" I stated, meeting her gaze as she stood before me. Her image, anyway. She had not even the nerve to set foot here. "Afraid, *Mother*? To face me here? Do I not even deserve an enemy-in-the-flesh?" I asked, mocking her.

"I could have brought him back!" she wailed plaintively.

"And brought destruction untold to all those you claim to love!" I responded. "I could not allow that. The price was too high."

"Never!"

"You can claim to love them, to love him, and not know that sometimes the price is too high?" I rejoined. "Begone, Mother. The Game is over."

"**NEVER!**" she shrieked, as I turned and walked away. I felt the blow hit me squarely in the back.

[*As Luc fell to a coward's blow I could not believe, mayhem reigned – and it was all we could do, Gabriel and the rest of us, to do what we knew he wanted.*

We stopped fighting. As one, we formed a protective barrier about him and refused to fight.

It grieved me to see her brought to this as she screamed and fought – but finally even her mind had to see the reality. The forces of both

Heaven and Hell aligned against her, protecting HIM.

She fell to her knees then.

"We'll take care of her," Peter and Paul said, leading her away.

"It's okay, Uncle Mike," Lucas said, appearing out of the smoke. "If you want to go."

I hesitated, feeling guilty, looking down at my friend. "I –"

"You need to sort things out. Make sure the right people take control. Go."

I obeyed. He spoke with Luc's voice.]

When I came to I was lying in my bed, on my belly. As I tried to move, I winced. Okay. Not a good idea. I felt cool hands on my flesh, cool liquid, and dozed. The next thing I remember is opening my eyes to see Hel by my side, cloth in hand. "Don't move," she said.

"Why not?"

"I'm going to give you a bed bath, and you'll soak the sheets, of course."

"I don't think so!" I exclaimed.

"Oh, don't be a baby. You haven't got anything we haven't seen before."

Phoenix! I struggled to rise only to find myself sat on. Now, at other times I might have found it a real turn on, if you know what I mean.

". . . and don't bellow, Lucifero diAngelus; it doesn't scare us."

"Call it payback, mister," Hel grinned mischievously.

Ah well, I thought, when surrender is inevitable, etc., etc. . .

"Okay, ladies . . . I'm all yours." I wasn't sure whether I was going to enjoy this or not. My back was still tender – but no longer an open wound. "Hel –"

"Hush. I know you didn't trust me. You weren't meant to, not entirely. Orders."

"Whose? For whom do you work?" I asked.

"Why, lover – who do you think?" purred Phoenix, laughing, as she sat beside me.

Yeah, right. Had to be. I had my spies, so it was only fair after all. I sighed. "Okay," I acknowledged. "Pax?"

"Pax," Hel responded, planting a kiss on my shoulder.

"Where's Lucas?" I asked, after what I thought was a few moments.

Phoenix laughed. "Redecorating, you might say."

"Can I get up?"

I sensed them looking at each other. "You can try. See how it goes."

Gingerly, I did so. I felt my bones and muscles object, but made it to my feet. I sat on the edge for a moment, then made it to my feet and headed for the mirror. I was naked, but as it had never concerned me before, it did not concern me now. I looked at the livid scar, like a lightening flash across the tan of my skin. A reminder of a mother's love, I thought acidly. I felt the tantalising kiss of silk against my flesh as Phoenix offered my scarlet silk robe to me. She helped me slip it on. I slipped an arm about her waist, drew her to me, and offered my free arm to Hel. Holding them both in my embrace, I breathed a sigh of relief – of release.

"Luc – satisfy my curiosity," Hel asked. "Where did you hide it?"

"Why, under the bed of course," I replied.

She laughed. "You –!"

"And now?"

I thought of that ancient Druidic stone circle in England – older than even those historians who thought they knew it all could ever dream. "Safe," I replied. They knew I would say no more.

"How DO you feel?" Phoenix asked.

"Better by the moment," I replied, a hand resting on her rear.

"Why – Luc!" Her hair brushed my skin and she laughed. Hel dug me in the ribs and joined in. Things might have got interesting, had a youthful voice not interrupted.

"Oh, ladies, do put him down. You can play with him later."

I looked at my son. He had not only been supervising the redecorating, I thought. "If you get any paint on my carpet –"

"I won't, I promise." I let the ladies go and walked towards him. "You look well – Father," he said, and threw himself against me. I winced, but enfolded him in my embrace anyway. What the hell, it was only pain. I could feel his tears, hot against my chest. That someone would weep – for me? I looked at Phoenix, a lump in my throat. She smiled, understanding.

"Come, Lucas – let us show your father what you've done." She eased him from me and led him by the hand. I followed, my movements becoming easier.

The Inferno had been beautifully redecorated. Ricky, as I entered, had a drink ready for me. I nodded my approval – of the drink, and everything else.

"Will it do?" Lucas asked. I heard the youthful eagerness in the nonchalant voice.

"Oh, I think so," I grinned. "And your room?"

"I'll show you later. Needs a few finishing touches."

"Okay." I supped. "What about a Grand Re-Opening?"

"Whatever you say." Ricky smiled. "Whenever you give the word."

"Lucas?" I asked.

"Yes?"

"Is it ready?"

"Yes. Yes – it is."

"Then set it up. Finish what you have so ably started."

He beamed with pride and straightened. Was it my imagination, or had he grown? "Yes, Father!"

My com-link buzzed, and I went to my office after excusing myself. "Yes, Jez?"

"It's not Jez – it's Mike."

"Oh. Sorry, Mike." Teach me to jump to conclusions. "What are you doing downstairs?"

"Delivering," he responded. He didn't volunteer what – I didn't ask. "I'm acting as intermediary, though. Adam wants a word."

"I bet he does. So do I. When and where?" I responded.

"Soon as you can. Name the place. He says he'll go anywhere."

I knew I could be vindictive if I chose – but there was no point in being childish. He hadn't done anything wrong – and nothing I wouldn't have done myself. I also knew where to find him.

"Tell him I'll be with him in a moment," I said. Mike chuckled, understanding.

"Will do. Out."

"Out."

I pursed my lips: looked at myself. What the hell, I thought . . . take me or leave me. So I strode this time into that pristine white environment, a livid blur of scarlet. It was worth it to see the faces of the upstairs staff as I sailed through barefoot, unshaven, in a blur of scattering cherubs, etc. Raphael grinned as I approached and opened the door for me.

Adam started as I entered, choking back a laugh. He rose, offered a hesitant hand to me. Should I play it up a little? Nah. I embraced him, acknowledging his companions.

"A moment in private, please," he asked, dismissing them. He waited, then gave a sigh and relaxed. "Luc –"

"Yeah?"

"Sorry."

I snorted. "Yeah . . . right!"

"This is just temporary – until we can have an election. I didn't do all this – for this – for the throne," he blurted.

I knew that. He could have had it any way. COULD have it now, for all I cared. No, that was not right. I **DID** care. I cared a lot.

"You'll do okay, Dam."

"And . . . the Ark?"

"Safe. Out of The Game. Trust me – if you want me to trust you," I said. "It's where no one can use it. It's – too wild a card to be allowed free." I shrugged. It was all the explanation I could or would give. If it was not enough – if he did not trust me after all this, he never would.

He studied me for a moment, and then nodded. "Good enough. How's the back?"

"Getting there. I'll have an interesting scar."

"Show me?" he asked.

I hesitated, wondering how many were watching on hidden cameras. I was tempted to give them a show. My eyes sparkled as I slipped it down over my back and turned for him. I could *really* shock them, I thought mischievously. I heard him gasp and turning to see him white-faced, promptly let the idea go. Another time.

"It's okay, Dam. Really."

"No – no, it's not okay," he whispered, tears in his eyes. "I never thought she would hurt you. Never. I would never have involved you if I had. I want you to believe me. You MUST believe me. She LOVES you!"

I snorted in derision. "Yeah. Some love. Don't worry about it – one more scar, what does it matter? If she loved me, it was only when it was convenient for her. When I was willing to play by her rules. Sorry, but I made my own a long time ago."

"I know. Still, if it matters, I'm sorry." I nodded. "Do you – want to see her?"

"No. Not – yet. Not until I can . . . forgive." I smiled, slipping my robe back into place. "You'll come to the re-opening, won't you? Lucas has been working very hard."

He smiled. "Try and keep me away. Let me know when."

"I will."

"And next time you visit, wear a pair of trousers, mm?" His eyes twinkled as he rounded the desk to embrace me briefly before I headed to the door.

I paused there. "Oh hell, Dam . . . I'm not even wearing underwear!"

His eyes widened as he realised what I had come close to doing, but I had opened the door before he could comment. His laughter followed me to the elevator.

Come one, come all and be welcome, I thought, standing at the top of the staircase that led down into the club. All was ready, and people were filtering in. The doors were open to any, but I was not expecting trouble. Not tonight, though Spike and Jude were on the doors just in case. Mike had sent a couple of his 'friends' down, *just in case.*

Hel and Phoenix were dressing, if basques and fishnets could be called 'dressing'; Chase, Morgan and the rest of the girls, similarly attired, were already on the dance floor or decorating the bar. Sex sells, especially here – and boy, were we going to 'sell' tonight. If Adam decided to raid the place, he'd better have arranged to have himself arrested, because he had one of my girls sat on his lap already, and they weren't having a polite conversation!

I grinned, glancing across at Lucas. He was dressed, like I was, in black leather trousers and white, silk shirt (although mine was looser fitting than his, and more open than closed). If I was going to dance, and I was, I needed all the freedom I could get. The Inferno was going to live up to its reputation tonight, I thought, as I watched The Fallen setting up and testing. Things were going to get **HOT**!

I saw Lucas's eyes widen and turned my head to see Phoenix and Hel approaching. "You're in for it, Father," he grinned wickedly.

"That's what I'm hoping for," I replied, straightening.

"Ready?" I asked, as they halted before me.

"Not quite," said Phoenix, glancing at Hel. "Something's not quite – right."

"Mmm . . ." she chuckled throatily, leaning against me. I could feel my hormones starting to race.

Phoenix chuckled in response and leaned against me, pulling my head to hers. When we separated, I looked more than a little ruffled, if you know what I mean.

"That's better."

"Much better," echoed Hel. "Don't bust your trousers, honey. Save it for later."

"HEL!" I glanced Lucas's way.

"Don't mind me," he grinned, walking to the stairs. "I'm all for education."

"Not that kind you're not!"

He pouted. "Spoilsport. Ready, ladies?"

"Ready!" they chorused, slipping their arms about my waist. What can a man do? I slipped mine around them and glared at my son.

"Showtime?" he asked.

I grinned. "Showtime."

He turned, raised his arms as a signal to below, and took his place a step below me. "Then let the show commence!"

The End . . .?

Welcome to Purgatory
The Game Continues

There's something therapeutic about sweeping floors. At least, that's what I was telling myself after a particularly heavy session at The Inferno. I could have left it to my staff, but that would hardly have been fair, seeing that I had contributed more than a little to the mess. But it had been one hell of a party!!!

Most of my staff were nursing sore heads. Indeed, my son was upstairs nursing what promised to be his first hangover.

I could have left things for later – locked the doors and hit the sack – but I was hyped up. Even if my nature had required sleep it would not have been forthcoming – so I decided to do a little 'housekeeping'.

I should have known better – been more alert . . . but the last thing I expected was the figure that walked through my door. My doors are, naturally, open to all, which occasionally invites trouble – but there's 'trouble', and there's TROUBLE.

She is TROUBLE.

Walks in, walks out, no strings, no cages. Tall, lithe as a cheetah, with short spiked white hair and violet eyes, that's Ashe.

They say that the female of the species is deadlier than the male – Ashe is proof if ever it were needed. Her lips are red as blood, her teeth as sharp as the blade she invariably wears. Ashe is a predator. Ashe is the best assassin I have ever met. Ashe is a vampire.

I stood looking at her, leaning on my broom in what I hoped was a nonchalant manner. She halted a few feet from me, as if uncertain of her reception. It had been a long time, and we had not parted on the best of terms. I could see the hilt of her sword revealed by her half open long coat. Some things never change.

I smiled. "Well, look what the wind blew in."

"Hello, Luc. It's been – a long time. Am I welcome?" she asked tentatively.

"If you come in peace and bring no vendettas to my door –"

"I promise," she replied, her voice still as husky as I remembered it. Could I trust her promise? I hoped so. Caution, however, would be useful.

"Then be welcome. Can I get you a drink?" I gestured to the bar.

"Sure."

"What'll it be? A, O, AB negative?"

"Ha ha!"

I poured myself a drink. I had a feeling I might need it. "So, what's new?" I asked.

"Nothing much."

I raised a brow. "Are you in trouble, Ashe?"

She sighed. "I'm always in trouble, honey, you know that." She hesitated. "Luc, I need a favour. Big time."

"As I thought – what's new?" I said, and saw a look in her eyes that unsettled me. Aw hell, I'm just a sucker for that 'lady in distress' look, even if it's Ashe. "What can I do for you?"

"I need a place to hide for a while. No questions asked."

"And no explanations, I suppose?" I met her gaze. I'm not a fool – I knew what I was taking on – and taking in. At least I thought I did. I sighed. "I'll find you a bed."

"Oh, any old wardrobe will do," she replied, deadpan. "You can hang me up with your trousers."

I snorted and laughed. "You used to try and get me out of my trousers."

"Well, a girl can always hope." She smiled over the rim of her glass.

Why did I feel that women were ganging up on me? Still, three of the loveliest women in creation hanging on my arm would do my reputation no harm whatsoever.

"Just check your weapon in, while you're here. You can have it back if you need it. Rules of the house."

"No problem," she replied, as if it was of no importance.

The fact that the sword was almost ageless, and priceless, and never left her side . . . still, nails as sharp as blades which could be enhanced at will did not exactly leave her powerless. I had felt those nails on my flesh on several occasions, I recalled with a smile. We had played dangerous games, in times past. Even given her nature, mine made me immune from harm – but there was thrill enough to add a certain – piquancy, if you know what

I mean. Perhaps you don't. Perhaps you would like to, or think you would. Believe me when I say it would be the last thing you, as a mortal, ever did.

I could reflect, as I walked, on the natures of the three women in my life at the moment. Hel was intrigue and volatility; Phoenix was, usually, a haven of calm; Ashe was danger incarnate. Life, I thought, was going to be interesting.

I ran into Phoenix, as I rounded a corner. Not literally. I move silently, but she usually knows when I am around. She stopped in time to avoid a collision.

"You look –" She paused, cocking her head to one side, pursing her lips. "Stimulated."

Her choice of words was interesting, to say the least. I grinned. "We have a visitor requesting sanctuary."

"We do? Who?"

"Ashe," I answered.

"Ashe?" Phoenix echoed, surprised. "Well, well! How is she? I haven't seen her in an age!"

"I'm not sure," I replied. "That she's come to ME for help, even if she won't say what the help is, is – interesting. You don't mind?"

Phoenix laughed softly. "Am I jealous, you mean? I learned a long time ago that being jealous of you, Lucifero diAngelus, is a useless exercise. The more anyone tries to tie you down, the less likely they are to succeed. We give you free rein, and we know you will always come back to us and we to you. We love you in our way, and we believe you love us in yours – as best you can. It is not a perfect solution, but we are not fools. One day, perhaps . . ." She leaned against me, ran a nail down my chest and kissed me lightly. "You sort out a bed – or a hanging space," she giggled, "and I'll go have a chat with Ashe."

Great, I thought. Girl talk. If they were going to be up talking, I was going to bed. "Okay."

I was listening to music (The Doors) in the darkness of my curtained bed, when I heard the doors open, followed the sound of giggles. Someone's been on the happy juice, I thought with a smile. The covers shifted, as the sound of Jim Morrison's voice pervaded my awareness. A husky voice asked, "What is your deepest desire, Lord of Darkness?" I heard Phoenix giggle as she slipped into bed.

Oh boy. Was I in trouble! "Now ladies . . ." I began.

"Yes, Lord?" Phoenix asked. I felt her laughter against my chest.

"Ladies, please . . .?"

"Please, what?" asked Ashe.

Oh . . . hell! "If you dig those nails into my back, I swear you'll find a stake through your heart!"

I felt her lips on my neck, and the gentle nip of her teeth. "Don't worry . . . I know all about that. Just – lie back and enjoy." I felt her nails on my belly, and a laugh became a groan.

"Be gentle with me." I surrendered.

I awoke to find myself alone in bed (to my relief!) and headed for the shower. I must be getting old, I thought, smiling. I caught a glimpse of my reflection in the mirror and laughed. I looked like the proverbial cat, I thought. Wrapping a towel about my waist, I strolled into my office. I thought I'd better check my messages. There were the usual calls to make, a few nuisance calls (no double glazing salesmen – you might be pleased to know there's a special Hell for double glazing salesmen. Any other nominations call 'Freephone Purgatory 666'). I'd get around to them, or put Jez on it. The only call, which troubled me, was from Adam. I'd have to return it, sooner or later. I knew why he was calling. I just wasn't ready or willing to respond.

"It's about Grandma, isn't it?"

I glanced in Lucas's direction. "Yes."

"And you'll feel bad if you go, and guilty if you don't."

A wise child, I thought. Don't laugh. I DO have a conscience (tell anyone, and I'll find you a vacancy with the double glazing salesmen!).

"Something like that." I looked him over. "How's the head?"

He grinned. "Okay. How's the back?"

"Fine," I responded, wondering what he knew. "Anything you need?"

"Oh. Yeah. Can I go riding with Mike and Phoenix?"

"Riding what?"

"I don't know. He didn't say."

"I don't see why not. Just be careful – and keep away from Storm."

"I will," he promised. Storm is my Hellsteed, and very particular who gets close. "Thanks. See you soon."

"Okay. Have a good day."

"I will. You too." He grinned and bounced out.

Oh for a child's energy, I thought wryly, stretching and deciding I'd better dress. I opened my wardrobe and stepped back in surprise. What the f**k? I swore. Hanging upside down in my wardrobe, wearing little more than a smile, was Ashe. Okay, when I stopped laughing I realised she was wearing a bodysuit. Her eyes opened and she smiled. I knelt and placed a kiss on her lips.

"Care to join me?" she invited lazily.

"I don't think it would stand the weight," I answered sceptically.

"Shame. You might find it – stimulating."

I needed very little stimulation, I thought, as she righted herself. She ran a finger lightly across my chest, tracing the outline of my tattoo. As she walked around me, I knew she was looking at the scar, still livid against my back. I felt her lips touch it, and her arms slide around my waist. You have work to do, I reminded myself. I could feel her, breathing against my back. Work. Yeah, right!

[I'd fled to Purgatory seeking sanctuary, and found myself in danger potentially greater than that from which I'd fled. The trouble is, Luc is temptation incarnate, and sexy as hell (if you'll excuse the pun). It's not his fault. He can't help it. It's just the way he is. He stands there wearing nothing but a towel and expects me to keep my hands to myself? I might be dead (well, undead), but I'm not stupid!]

"Purgatory 666," I answered my phone drowsily.

"Don't you ever answer your phone?" I heard my brother ask.

"I just did," I replied, sitting up and brushing the hair from my face.

He chuckled. "What have you been doing, brother dear?" he asked, and I cursed as Ashe sat up beside me. I reached out and shut off the web-cam. "Spoilsport!" he said.

"What can I do for you?" I asked, knowing.

"Are you sure you're not too busy?" he asked mischievously.

I laughed, and felt Ashe's lips on my shoulder. I shrugged and murmured, "Not now, Ashe. Business."

She took the hint. "Okay. Shall I go?"

"I don't think it's private – is it, Dam? Let me guess, Mother dearest requests my presence."

"I'm not sure I would put it *that* way. Her words were more 'If he can tear himself away from his whores' . . . – sorry, Ashe."

"I've been called worse," she responded.

". . . have him come to ME," he concluded. "And that's the polite version."

I paused for a moment. "Do I **have** to?"

"Of course not. I just thought you might want to look her in the eye one last time, as a sort of closure – if only to spit in it."

That was Dam, I thought, ever the peacemaker, the mediator. The fixer. There was no way, I thought, he was ever going to be able to fix **this**.

I felt Ashe's hand on my arm. "I could go with you," she whispered.

I smiled. "Thanks, but I doubt they'd let you through the gates." The thought of Ashe striding through the holier-than-thou Domain upstairs cheered me no end. It might be possible, if Dam would allow a special dispensation. The thought was decidedly delicious. "I'll let you know when I'm ready," I told both of them.

"Fair enough." I heard the understanding in his voice. We chatted about inconsequential inter-realm matters before saying our goodbyes.

After attending to business 'downstairs', I returned to The Inferno to find Lucas and Mike giving the girls their briefing. I left them to it and went to find out who was still 'home'. Hel, I was told, had gone 'shopping', leaving Phoenix and Ashe behind.

"You didn't fancy a trip?" I enquired.

"Not this time," Phoenix replied. "Nothing I need right now."

"Oh. See you downstairs?"

"In a little while," she said. "Oh, and by the way – Lucas knows about Ashe being here."

Ah. I should have thought about that. Not used to having a son around was my excuse. Phoenix understood. I could see her amusement.

"Don't worry, Luc. No problems."

By that, I assumed that she meant that Ashe would be as careful about Lucas as he would be around her. (Vampires exude a certain *glamour* (in the ancient sense) – they can't help it. It's what often draws their victims to them. Purgatory tended to negate that influence due to its special nature, but – to put it bluntly – Ashe was a looker even when you were unaware of her nature, and my son was growing fast . . . know what I mean?)

"Okay."

I changed and went back into the club.

Lucas wandered over to join me at the bar. "You don't mind –" He gestured towards the girls.

"No. It's good you take an interest."

"I'm learning from the master." He gave me a mock salute.

I laughed.

"Talking of ladies –"

"Phoenix and Ashe will be down shortly," I responded. "Talking of Ashe –"

"Yes?"

"Be careful. She's –"

"It's okay, Dad. It's cool. We introduced ourselves earlier. I found her hanging in your wardrobe." I had not thought to ask Phoenix if Lucas had actually MET Ashe yet, I realised. I was going to have to tighten up my act.

"Ah."

"I asked her if that was her usual resting place. She told me it was a joke. I asked her if she wouldn't be more comfortable waiting for you in your bed. She suggested I try it her way, she'd already tried mine . . ."

". . . I get the idea!" I interrupted hastily, before it got embarrassing. "Dad?" I asked suddenly. "DAD??"

He yelped laughter and scrambled away. I took up the chase, and came to a halt almost on top of him.

Ashe and Phoenix were stood at the top of the staircase, wearing skin-tight leather catsuits – Ashe in black, Phoenix in white. They looked – sensational.

"Holy shit!" Lucas exclaimed. I clipped him around the ear. "OW!"

"Language!"

He grinned at me. He was right, though. They looked **HOT**.

"If you're thinking what I think you're thinking, you're too young to be thinking it!"

He grinned at me. "Age is relative, Father . . . this is Purgatory after all. Don't worry, they're all yours. I'm going to play pool. Have fun."

"I intend to," I murmured, extending my hands to my ladies, escorting them to the bar.

"Hey, Luc – join us!" called Gabe from the dais. I don't usually perform (at least not while I'm sober) . . . but why not? I heard a burst of applause as I shook out my hair and took up my best Jim Morrison pose. Time tomorrow for work – tonight was for pleasure. Sex and drugs and rock 'n' roll. Well, that's what it's supposed to be like, right?

Well believe me, we know how to have a good time. I may not perform often but when I do, the audience knows it. Tonight, I was hot. I was not the only one with hormones raging, I thought wryly. I could play the game too. Tomorrow, I would be the businessman, the Lord of Darkness. Tomorrow, I might even pay a visit to my mother.

Tonight, however, I would be whatever they wanted me to be. If they could turn ME on, I could do the same to them. Turnabout is fair play, after all!

I hoped Adam's spies did not report to him and decide to raid us, I grinned. Otherwise, things could get very INTERESTING.

Am I ruled by my emotions? No more than anyone, whatever impressions I might give. I can be as cold and calculating as the next, more so. I have done many things I have not been proud of but which have been necessary . . . but I DO like to put on a performance. Showtime, and all that . . . and if I was going to face my mother, I might be putting on the performance of my life. Whatever impression I might give about the relationship between the two of us, it was not always this way. In the beginning, it was good. We DID love one another once, before – before The Fall.

When did it turn bad? I'm not sure when it started. Whether there was one occasion that started it all. Perhaps it was inevitable. Perhaps it was part of some even greater design.

I only knew I could not toe her line, walk in her shadow. I had to be my own man, so to speak. She was used to power by then, enjoyed it. A democratically elected and ruled Domain? Yeah, right!

Okay, perhaps I'm no better. But then, I'm not supposed to be, am I? No matter what 'that Book' says, she was never an *angel*. (Okay, bad pun I know!) You should have seen her the day she 'kicked me out'! Talk about turning the air blue! The curses she screamed at my back made even ME blush! Poor Mike, having to 'escort me off the premises' . . . it was Mike I felt sorry for, and Raphael. They had to cast me out, as the saying goes, their friend, and go back and face the music. Listen to her raging, listen to the things she said about me, knowing the truth. Perhaps it had been the beginning of the affliction that held her now.

Had it been my fault? It would have been so easy to blame myself. Perhaps some responsibility had to be mine – *I* had been no angel. Believe me, I know that. I was not without fault. I am not casting all the blame on her. Yes, I had contemplated rebellion – but only because I sensed what was happening to her. The beginnings of madness, if you want to put it that way. The seeds of illness. I did not want power upstairs then, and I never have. An eternity of harps, fluffy clouds and choral music? That's MY idea of Hell, not Heaven!!!

Yet, despite it all, my friends had stood by me. Phoenix, Mike, Gabe, Peter, Paul, Raphael . . . and countless unnamed others. They had known the truth, and kept the peace. For them, I had to think carefully how I faced her. I did not want to make things worse than they already were, no matter what my feelings might be. What I would say might well depend on what she said to ME. There might, at the last, be nothing to say at all.

While I had no desire to be childishly antagonistic, neither was I going to go against my nature and appear meek and mild. I stood looking in my wardrobe (not containing an inverted Ashe this time) and frowned. How often had I heard the ladies complain "But I haven't a *thing* to wear"? I knew how they felt.

I sensed Phoenix at my back and felt her fingers caress my neck. "If you want company –"

I smiled. "Ashe offered too."

"I know."

I was tempted to be defiant. I was tempted to march into 'Heaven' with 'my whores' at my back and say "Screw you" to her . . . but Adam occupied the hot seat now – until the elections at least (and, I suspected, beyond that) – and while I might wish to soothe my own ego, there was a certain protocol to be observed.

"No thanks, babe. I have to do this alone."

"Sure?"

"No." I laughed. I wasn't sure at all. "But that's the way it will be. Okay – so, what do I wear?"

"Poor baby!" she chuckled. "Move aside – let me look."

"Can I help?" asked Ashe, pushing me gently aside. I sighed dramatically and went to sit on my bed while they went through my wardrobe. It was almost embarrassing to hear "What about

. . .", "You've got to be joking", "too old", "too flashy", etc. I had
the feeling that, like Hel, I needed to go shopping!

In the end, they settled on a simple white shirt and black
trousers combination. (Actually, it's quite a common theme in my
wardrobe, in a variety of styles. I think I might be becoming too
predictable!) I tied back my hair, hung a bootlace tie around my
neck.

"Do you want me to come in with you?" Adam asked, as we
halted outside the door of Gaia's Tower. I looked up at The Tower
– part of 'The Mansion' yet separate. Secure. A prison.

"No, Dam. It's okay."

"I'll be watching. Just in case. If you're sure . . .?"

"I'm sure," I said – but I lied. The last thing I actually wanted
to do was enter The Tower. I heard the door lock behind me
and climbed the spiral staircase. No obvious security, but none
was needed. Cameras watched every step, and sensors every
movement. I heard a further click as the door at the top opened
to admit me. The room was simple but elegant. No need for a
'padded cell' unless she gave them cause.

She was sitting in a rocking chair, sewing. At least, that's what
it looked like. I was not certain she even knew of my presence,
until she spoke.

"So – you came, Lucifer."

"As you see." I looked round for a seat and pulled up a stool.
"How are you? You look . . . well." Lord, but I sounded inane!

"I am well."

"Is there anything you need?" I asked.

"Freedom," she replied, setting down her sewing and looking
at me. "You came alone . . . I did not think you would?"

"Whom did you expect?" I enquired. "My whores?" Sarcasm
dripped into my voice. I could not help it.

"He told you that?"

"He did."

"He always was – honest."

"You make it sound dirty, Gaia," I responded. "Of course I
came alone. Why should I subject anyone else to this ordeal?"

"So you admit you did not want to come."

"Of course I do!" I laughed bitterly. "You no more wish for my
presence here than I to be here."

"Then why DID you come?"

"I'm damned if I know," I admitted. "But then, I'm damned anyway, am I not?"

"You could have had EVERYTHING!" she said, leaning earnestly towards me.

"I have everything I want," I replied.

"Do you? Are you sure?"

"Quite sure. I never wanted to be your puppet, any more than Adam does . . . or Jayce did."

"You're just like your father," she sneered. "Weak."

I smiled. "Yes, I'm just like my father. We both walked out on you to live our own lives. You'll never forgive either of us for that, will you? For escaping your clutches?"

"I wanted what was best for you!"

"You wanted what was best for YOU!" I shouted, hissing behind my teeth and calming myself. Dam was going to have a nice little entertainment, at this rate. "There's no point in my staying, is there? We really have nothing to say to each other." I rose to leave.

"I have plenty to say to you!" she shouted at my back. "You WILL come back, one day! You'll do what I want in the end."

I laughed. "When Hell freezes over, perhaps. Father was right – you're just a conniving bitch!"

"Just like your whores."

"At least my 'whores' give me more love than you ever did," I said.

"Love? You don't know what the word means!"

"Oh, I think I have more idea than you do, Mother dear."

"You'll crawl back to me, you bastard. I'll have you kneel at my feet! I'll have you beg . . ." As she lurched for me, I caught her wrists. My eyes blazed with a fury I could barely control as I looked into her eyes.

"You'll have me beg for what, MOTHER? The kind of love YOU give?" I pushed her from me, unfastening my shirt and turning my back. "IS THIS WHAT YOU MEAN BY LOVE?" I faced her again. "Forgive me if I gracefully decline."

I sketched a theatrical bow and headed for the door. She screamed and lurched for me. I felt her nails touch me and lost control. I whirled about and pushed her across the floor with all the force I could muster.

"Touch me once more, and it will be the last thing you EVER do."

I left her in a heap and slammed the door behind me. Outside its confines, I leaned against it, dishevelled, trying to control my breathing and my temper, knowing all the while that Adam was watching (and probably half his staff), that they had seen me lose control, and not giving a damn.

I looked up at the camera. "Sorry, Dam. You tried."

Then I descended the stairs as fast as I could and headed 'home'. At least there, I hoped, I would find a welcome.

My bruised ego was eased a little when I walked back into my bedroom. There was laughter coming from the bathroom and packages on the bed, which bespoke Hel's return. Curious, I headed in that direction. I found the bathroom lit by a blaze of candles, champagne chilling, and the jacuzzi occupied by three lovely ladies – and my son! Only the fact that one of those ladies was his mother kept me from jumping to conclusions.

"Successful shopping expedition?" I asked.

"We won't know until we see you dressed," Phoenix grinned. "We sent Hel on a clothes hunt for you. New image."

"Oh really."

"Come on, Dad, chill out," grinned my son. "Drop 'em."

"Have you been drinking?" I enquired, arching an eyebrow.

"Just a little," he admitted. "Honest."

I frowned at his mother and disrobed. "BAD example."

"Pot calling the kettle black," retorted Phoenix as I slipped in.

What had they come up with, I wondered? If Lucas had any hand in it, I dreaded to think. I studied the contents of the boxes apprehensively. The leather trousers were laced up the sides and looked like they belonged in a bondage club. There was a vest to match (which caused me a bad case of the hiccups). The other combination had a shirt with frills – very Beau Brummell!

O-kay.

For a few moments, I actually contemplated cutting my hair (then I wouldn't have to wear a bow!). Then I came up with an idea. There used to be a heavy metal band called Kiss. You might have heard of them. Gave me a LOVELY idea for makeup! It also gave me a wonderful idea for a theme night!

"Was it – very bad?" asked Phoenix, as we prepared for the 'evening'.

"Bad enough," I replied. I gave a brief synopsis. I saw them glance at each other, then at Lucas.

"What?" he asked. "What?? I'm not a fool, you know. I know what's going on. Grandma's going bats."

"I'm not sure I'd put it quite that way!" Ashe complained indignantly.

Lucas grinned. "No offence intended."

"I'll excuse you. THIS time."

She scowled at him; he made the sign of a cross with his fingers. I scowled at him, and we lunged for him together, colliding on the bed and ending up in a heap on the floor. Disentangling ourselves from the silk sheets, we skidded after him, hurtling down the corridor at his heels and towards the staircase with Phoenix bringing up a more dignified rear. Lucas yelped laughter, slid down the staircase banister and launched himself into Mike's waiting arms as we descended in a more normal fashion. Mike tossed Lucas onto his feet and did his best to delay us. The chase continued over tables, seats and the bar until eventually I ended up flying along the bar and tackling him behind the potted palm.

"OOF!"

"Serves you right," I gasped.

"Get – off me."

"Please." As a parent it was my duty to teach him manners, wasn't it?

"Please!"

I groaned and rolled over. Sitting up, I glared at him, Mike and Ricky (who at least had the brains to placate me with a drink). Ashe was nowhere in sight – nor was Phoenix. I was sat on the floor, barefoot and bare-chested with my hair half over my face, when Dam walked in. He halted in front of me, a quizzical expression on his face.

"I came to see if you were okay," he said, offering a hand to me.

I grimaced and rubbed the base of my spine. "I'm not sure," I answered. "I think I'm leaking."

"Pardon?"

"Ouch!" I removed the broken jar from beneath my rear. With luck, it would only be a scratch. I tried to look, and he laughed.

"Unless you've got green blood, I think you'll survive."

"And you thought leather was just kinky," I laughed.

"I think I said YOU were just kinky," he replied, the broad grin on his face fading. "Seriously."

"Seriously – I should not have lost my temper with her."

"Only natural, in the circumstances."

"Did I hurt her?"

"Physically? No. Psychologically? I doubt it. It's YOU I'm worried about."

"Oh, I'll bounce back, Dam. I usually do. Drink?"

"Thanks."

"Ricky?" I prompted.

He smiled. "Coming right up."

We took our drinks to a booth. "What can I do for you?" I asked. "You could have enquired after my health without a personal visit. Not that it's not appreciated . . ."

He smiled in acknowledgement. "It's a little embarrassing."

"Ah!" I could guess. "You want me to keep a low profile until the election is over."

"Something like that."

"It either is, or it isn't," I pointed out.

"Luc!"

"Okay, okay!" I raised my hands. "I'll try . . . but I ought to point out, in my defence, that you invited ME."

"I know," he sighed. "But in MY defence, I felt I had to try. I'm sorry it didn't work – but I'm not sorry I tried." Politics, I thought. "Don't worry, it will all be over soon."

"I hope so."

"It's not for me, it's for all of us."

Yeah, how many times had I heard that over the years? Still, I had my own troubles. Such as getting around to asking Ashe why she HAD come to Purgatory. Why now? That was a good question. More to the point, given the past, what could scare Ashe enough to cause her to flee TO me?

"Yeah, yeah, you've heard it before. I know. But a friend upstairs is useful; surely even you will admit that."

"It'll make a nice change," I acknowledged.

He sipped his drink and settled back lazily. "Besides, I had to get out of the place for a while. You're quite a topic of conversation, you know."

"That's unusual?" I enquired laconically.

"Well, it's not everyday you perform a striptease in front of half The Mansion's staff."

I grimaced. "I didn't exactly plan it."

"Just as well," he grinned impishly. "I don't think I could cope with all the casualties if you walked through wearing anything less. It gives me an inferiority complex."

"Don't give me ideas," I mumbled. "I'm considering having a 'heavy metal' themed party night in the near future – probably after the election – open invitation . . . if you or any of your staff want to come?"

"Sounds good. I could do with letting my hair down a bit."

"You'll need to grow it, first." I eyed him.

"Oh, I think you've more than enough to go around," he replied.

"I was thinking of cutting it."

"Oh, I rather think the ladies like you just the way you are. I gather they like to run their hands through your hair – or something."

It was the 'or something' that worried me. "It was just a thought. Bad hair day, and all that. Can I get you another drink?"

"No – I'd better get back. Thanks, though – for the drink, and the invitation."

"No problem."

I watched him leave. I had a feeling it was going to be a quiet night, so I asked Ricky to take charge and told him to page me if he needed backup. I went to my office, did a little paperwork, and then called Ashe to me.

"Tell me the truth, this time. Why did you walk out without a word?" I asked, as she pulled up a chair.

She looked down at her hands. "Do you remember what I said?"

"Oh, I remember. Right after I'd asked you to stay with me, you told me that you were the assassin I'd been looking for – and that the person who'd paid your contract was my ever-loving mother."

She winced. "What I did not tell you – could not tell you – was the clause in my contract that covered my failure to deliver."

"Go on," I urged softly.

"Do you know what a 'Soul Chaser' is?"

I frowned. "A demon sent to retrieve a reluctant or 'difficult' soul."

"Close enough. Well, to put it simply – she would put a 'Chaser' on me if I failed to kill you."

"So you fled," I whispered.

"Yes, I fled. It's been after me ever since, Luc."

I cursed. "Why did you not say something? Why did you not come to me before?"

Ashe sighed. "I thought I could handle it. Thought – does it matter? I can't handle it alone – and I can't run any more. I needed time to – gather my courage for one last fight."

I could guess the courage it had take for her to say that. Ashe was proud, and a consummate artist, if such a phrase could be used. There were few her equal with a blade, and fewer her superior. If she couldn't handle it . . .

"And you came here because it can't harm you here. Neutral territory."

She bowed her head, and whispered, "I'm sorry."

I slipped out from behind my desk, raising her head gently and saw blood-tears in her eyes. I knelt and kissed her gently. "What changed?"

"I received a note saying the rules had changed. That it would take me WHEREVER I fled. I've been trying to find a way to tell you – or leave you again."

I crushed her to me, held her so hard a lesser person would have been begging for mercy – as thoughts tumbled through my mind.

"If it violates the Compact of Neutrality here, it's fair game. Even if Mike's not here, I'm not without my resources," I said, after some moments. "There has to be some way to stop it – if it comes . . . and we have to presume it will. I'll have a word with Mike – if he doesn't have any answers, he'll know who will." I stood up, pulling her to her feet. "I know you consider yourself an 'independent woman', but we all need friends – and we ARE your friends. If for no other reason than that, we'll do what we can."

Only one person can cancel a contract, and that was the person who took it out in the first place . . . and my mother was hardly likely to cooperate! In fact, in some part of her twisted mind, she was probably aware of the irony of it. She would get me out of the way, if Ashe fulfilled her contract, and if I stepped between Ashe and the Soul Chaser, it would either a) take me (if it could), or b) get me out of the way for a seriously long time, or c) hit me where it hurt by taking Ashe and anyone else who got in its way.

Could it take me out – permanently? I was not sure. I am special, being Lord of Darkness – as Adam would be 'special', if he permanently took the seat upstairs, as my opposite number. I'm not just being arrogant – it's just the way it works. It's not exemption from rules, exactly, just a certain bending of them, kind of. But it *could* seriously weaken me – and if I was out of the way . . . well, Hell is full of those who would like to take my place given half a chance. If I lost my 'position', would I lose that which made me 'special', so to speak? Well, some of it. Some of it comes with the 'office' . . . some of it from other sources. That did not concern me now. The only thing that concerned me was how I was going to handle this. I realised I did not have the faintest idea. So I did what I always do when I need that kind of answer – I sent for Mike. I could have asked Spike, or Jude – they're my Enforcers, after all, and Spike's my 'Sifter' – but when it comes down to it, they're not Michael.

[I was not sure what Luc's reaction was going to be when I 'came clean' – Luc might appear frivolous sometimes, but he's not. He's as hardheaded as they come when it comes to a fight. He doesn't leave his friends out in the cold – which was why I'd come back. No matter what I'd done . . . and I knew I'd hurt him badly that day a long time ago . . . but I'd been – well – younger then, and sure I could handle anything that came. Flattered? Yes . . . that the Lord of Hell should feel anything for ME? Luc doesn't give a portion of his heart easily . . . but neither does he turn away a friend, whatever they did to him. He might not like me to say it, but he's as honourable in his way as anyone I've ever met – and I'd trust him more than most. WAS trusting him, after all.

Did I expect him to welcome me back, when I walked back through his door as if I'd never been away? No, I did not. Luc might be generous of heart, but if the mood takes him he can be as vindictive as the next person. He's not wholly virtuous (or he'd be sitting upstairs, wouldn't he?) – he has his faults . . . but he will let you lean on him, draw strength from him, and not hold it against you. Not throw what some might term a weakness back in your face. Ask him for help, admit you have a problem, and he'll do his best to help – or, if he cannot, help you find someone who can . . . but foul up an operation, say you can do something you cannot do, and then he might, if the mood took him, find some way to make you pay. Luc is never entirely predictable. Well, except where his mother is concerned.

Why, then, you ask, if I feel for him what I do, did I take the contract against him? Allow me to explain. Back then (and this is a LONG time ago) I was arrogant enough to believe I COULD. I thought I could play both sides of the game. Could not resist the price. Thought that it did not matter who was Lord of Hell . . . that one was as good as another. After all, vampires such as I are a step out of line too – neither alive or dead, human and non-human – special, you might say, just as he is. Perhaps some part of me from my non-vampire past believed that he was EVIL, and believed what I was told about him . . . until I met him. Until I saw a side of him that few ever see. Phoenix might be one of the select few too. Certainly those few might be counted on the fingers of one hand. Sure, he can be funny, and sexy as hell . . . but it's more than that. I'm not really sure I can explain quite what. Do I love him? I suppose I do, inasmuch as my kind can love. Would it hurt me, if he were hurt FOR me? You bet your ass it would!

So I watch him talking with Mike, listen to them discussing things and try to keep my mind in focus. This is serious, I tell myself. You aren't even sure you HAVE a soul . . . don't they say that vampires are soulless? But if that's so, why did she put a contract on you for your soul to be taken? What would happen if my supposed soul was taken . . . would I exist as a mindless thing? I suspected that might be so, given the way Mike was looking at me . . . and that could not be a good thing. I would have to exact a promise from him to put an end to my existence, should that happen. (Mike, that is, not Luc. Mike was more likely to comply with my wishes and understand the asking.)

I should be concentrating, not letting my mind wander.]

" . . . we can do for the moment," Luc said, looking askance at me. I tried to look as if I had been listening, but knew he suspected I hadn't.

"I'll get right on it," Mike promised. "Can I use your office?"

"Help yourself. I'm going downstairs for a drink. I think I need one. Coming Ashe?"

"Unless Mike needs any help?"

Mike looked up from the console and smiled. "Er, no, it's okay, Ashe. You look like you need a drink."

"Can I get you anything?"

"You can send something up later – ask Ricky for a few snacks, if he's in a good mood."

"Will do."

I led Ashe downstairs. I had a feeling she needed a broader spectrum of company than mine at the moment, and left her with Hel and some of the girls. I needed to go 'downstairs' for a while.

I braced myself as I crossed the reception area; I could see someone coming towards me that heralded trouble. If he'd blown up another computer . . .

He grinned. "Hi, boss."

"What have you done this time, Rod?" I asked.

Herod grinned cheerfully. "Nothing, boss . . . not a thing. Just feeling a little bored – thought you might have a job for me?"

"I might at that," I responded, thoughtfully. Whatever else he was, Rod was something akin to genius where research was concerned. "Come with me. I have a little research project in mind that would suit you to a T."

I left him researching Soul Chasers while I went to check out things in The Pit. The Pit, I should explain, is the downstairs equivalent of The Inferno . . . but they get away with things in there that even *I* would not risk. More often than not when I'm not there, of course. Or at least, I have been known to turn a blind eye. It's sometimes a useful source of information, you might say. If there was no one interesting to talk to, I usually wandered back into my office and watched from the comfort of my chair. Tonight, it was more a matter of whom I did not want to see. I was in no mood for the 'You should spend more time down here than up there' lobby. Probably I should, but I liked my life just the way it was – and as long as no one complained, and if things ran smoothly, I saw no reason to change things.

With both brains working on the matter, it was not long before the data poured in and I could settle down to plan. There was conflict, of course – because Chasers are an independent lot, outside the control of either Domain, and somewhat secretive. The data was a little unclear as to how to dispose of one, as it's not the sort of thing that they like to advertise. I had a feeling I was going to have to wing it.

Well, if there's anything I'm good at, it's improvisation.

The Compact, however, forbade chasing on neutral ground. If he was coming HERE (and I believed he was) he had to believe he could take me out. And Michael. AND Ashe. He had to believe he was very good indeed. Or that I would stand aside. Or both.

Either that or he had a death wish, I thought.

I should explain – that's not as crazy as it sounds. Some Chasers are under a geis – a compulsion – to perform their grim task. Few, after all, would do it willingly. That being said, some do – and in all cases they cannot be bought and they cannot be stopped. Legend says they cannot be destroyed . . .

. . . But then, they also said the Titanic was unsinkable.

I'd just have to prove them wrong, wouldn't I?

Yet, no matter what I read, and what I thought I knew, nothing could prepare me for the call that brought me from my office to the dance floor.

I took time to dress – my trademark white shirt and black leather trousers; put on my full-length black leather coat; strapped on my longsword with its dragon-tooled hilt. I had not worn 'Slayer' in a long time. I wore it now for effect – damn the rules – I would use it if I must.

If there was anyone in the large room, I did not see them. Did not wish to acknowledge any. Did not want to shift my gaze from him.

All I could think was, The bitch. The bitch!! as I crossed the room and halted before him. Much could depend on the next few moments – or it could make no difference at all.

Our eyes met, and he took my measure. He rose and faced me. If he was taller than I, it was not evident. The years had been kinder to him than the geis, or so it seemed. A geis, it is said, rides a man hard, if his service is unwilling, and his eyes were haunted as he looked into mine.

"If you hunt here, it is against both the Compact and my will," I said, in a cold voice barely recognisable as my own.

"I have come – for the creature known as Ashe," he replied. "She broke her contract. The price must be paid."

"There is sanctuary here for those who ask it," I responded, equally formal. My tongue felt thick in my mouth. Some cool dude, huh?

"I can be patient."

"You will have need to be."

"She will not remain forever. No one ever does. Sooner or later, she will step beyond your protection. Or tire of you. Your women always do."

That was my mother talking. "Is that so? We shall see. I, too, can be patient."

"Then you have learned much. It was never one of your virtues."

"I was not aware I had any," I responded mockingly. "At

least according to her." I sketched a bow. "I bid you respect the Compact."

I turned, and walked away, feeling my back naked. It would have ended there, I think, at least for the moment, had Lucas not come through the door. He did not see my companion, until it was too late. In a blur of motion, the Chaser's blade was at Lucas's throat. A voice screamed fury; I knew it for mine.

"Surrender the vampire, or his blood will flow."

I looked at the blade at my son's throat, met his eyes. He was calm, surprisingly, as I drew Slayer.

[I have never felt so scared – or so calm. I've never seen a look in anyone's eyes that I saw in his – yet I can't even say what it was: anger, fear, love, passion and ice-cold calm. The blade in my father's hand seemed to glow with a life of its own. I did not feel the blade at my throat, only the force of my father's personality, willing me to be still, to trust him. He smiled, cold and deadly, and when he spoke, his voice was soft and heavy with promise and menace.]

"If one drop of his blood is spilled, I swear that no one and no barrier will prevent my tearing her heart from her body with my bare hands," I said quietly. "What she lays against me, I will bear . . . but if she causes harm to my son . . ."

"Your – son . . .?"

The pressure of the blade on his throat eased enough for Lucas to slip free, and he did – a little inelegantly, but style is not everything.

"Yes. My son. YOUR GRANDSON – FATHER!!"

Lucas froze in shock – which is just as well, as Ashe flew down from the balcony onto the floor between us. I lunged, flung her out of the way, and flung out my arm to prevent her passing. I felt the impact shoot through my body and turned so that I could keep an eye on both of them, and stood with my arms outstretched.

"Enough!" I roared. "Ashe – enough. Spill blood, and I can't protect you!"

"But – Lucas!"

"I know," I said, quieter.

"It's alright, Ashe." Lucas caught her arm. "Please."

There was sympathy in her eyes as she looked at me – a premonition, perhaps? – but she lowered her blade and her head.

"As you wish, my Lord."

I saw Phoenix's arms enfold her son and draw him back, and Ashe retreat back, giving me a clear field should I need it – and I would. I knew it, and my gathering audience knew it.

I could see the pain on his face, knew the geis was taking a hold, overriding any natural feelings, and traces of the man he had once been.

He raised his blade, and I raised mine. There are times when Slayer takes on a life of its own. This was one. I was simply its instrument. How long the battle lasted I do not know. I lost all track of time. Perhaps there is such a thing as genetic memory, but in simple terms, our bodies knew each other well. We had matched blades before, but never in earnest. The difference now was that some part of him did not want to take me down, part of him wanted to die. He knew, in some part of his mind that was still his own, that Slayer was the one weapon that **COULD**. In one moment, I looked down into his eyes. My hair was wild over my face, and sweat dripped from my face onto his. My chest heaved with exertion, as did his.

"Kill me," he begged, his eyes wholly his own. "While you can. It's the only way."

I hesitated. I knew I could do it. Must do it, if there was to be any future worth having – because if he gave in to it, there would be no other ending. I could take him out of the equation, into that no-place that is out of time, until such a time as he could heal, or be released – or until bit by bit he faded away into the matter from which we all come – or until a 'cure' could be found. (For there was no way, I knew, that SHE would release him. Her revenge for his courage to leave her.)

"With love, if you can," he whispered.

I screamed in pain as Slayer slid, almost of its own will, into his heart. I knelt there for some time, the only sound my ragged breathing, until finally I staggered to my feet and wiped the blade on his shirt.

"Take him. Do what must be done," I said to no one, but Michael knew the words were for him. Dimly, I was aware of Ashe moving towards me, of Phoenix pulling her back, saying "Let him go" as I walked past, blade in hand.

They found me some time later, curled up in the shower, water tumbling over me as if to wash away what I had done. I was in shock, I learned later – does that surprise you? It shouldn't. When a blood lust high sends you crashing, you crash hard.

I did not resist as they undressed me – Phoenix, Hel and Ashe – and threw my ruined clothes into a heap on the floor for later disposal; nor did I resist as they dried me off and led me to bed.

"Luc? Lucifer? Can you hear me?" Phoenix asked. I did not answer. "He's freezing!"

They tried to warm me.

"Leave me," I mumbled.

"Not on your life, Lucifer diAngelus! You need us."

"I want to be alone," I insisted.

"Sorry, honey, no go. I know you. I know what you want to do . . . but it's not the right time."

She was right, I thought dimly, drowsily. Revenge, as the Chinese say, is a dish best eaten cold. I could feel the warmth returning to my limbs. I smiled languorously. I had three beautiful ladies in my bed, I thought . . . and, as Scarlett O'Hara might say, tomorrow is another day . . .

The end . . . ?
Not yet!

Welcome to Purgatory
Endgame

While I rested, word of what I had done reverberated through the Domains. While it would do my reputation no harm, I had no desire to become a target for anyone who wanted to take me on – take me down – whatever. Downplay was the order of the day – at least until the upstairs elections were over. Light body armour when I went out and about might be the just what the doctor ordered too.

I had been avoiding Dam like the proverbial plague – but I could not do so forever. I called him, and was relieved when he was engaged . . . but he called me back almost immediately.

"How are you feeling?" he asked. "You look okay."

"Could be worse. Dam – I had no choice."

He smiled sadly. "I know. Luc – I have a favour to ask – and you won't like it."

I knew what he was going to ask – and what my response would be. One more item on the account which my mother (our mother) would be called to pay.

"Ask, then," I responded, my voice chilling. I saw the pain in his eyes.

"I need to ask you not to harm her. She's mad, Luc. Not accountable for her actions."

I sighed. "She was not mad when she began this – and I'm not entirely sure she is now. She's quite an actress. All she wants, all she ever wanted, is to tear us apart. One of her sons in the hot seat after her. Looks like she's getting what she wants after all." My voice dripped poison, and I cursed myself.

"Luc – Don't do this. PLEASE!" he begged.

"I'm sorry, Dam. I can't give you a promise, beyond the one that I'll do nothing before the election." I smiled faintly. "Who knows? My conscience might get the better of me, and I might decide she's not worth it."

"I'll pray for that," was his reply. "I don't want war between us, Luc . . . but if you come after her on our soil, that's what you will be declaring. Then she'll win, Luc. Think on it. That way, SHE'LL WIN. Out."

I looked at the blank screen and sighed. He was right – damn him. He was right. But what if I could get her out of there? (Had he been hinting at that, perhaps?) If not here, then somewhere – anywhere – where I could deal with the thirst for revenge that burned in my gut.

An eye for an eye – her code.

Revenge is mine, sayeth the Lord – mine.

Yet, I could also see that it might be the very thing she wanted. Her blood also on my hands. Her legend, then, would be unassailable, both in the Domain upstairs and without. Ah, what a tangled web we weave, etc.

In the cold light of day, I could take a step back. Seek some way to satisfy all sides. Without bringing on a war!

The election came and went almost without notice, in the end. Oh, there was a little rallying going on that filtered down, a few posters stuck on walls. A few broadcasts canvassing support – the usual stuff, which I was able to ignore.

I had enough to think on for a time, getting ready for our party. Re-decorating had taken some effort, but we were ready. I had even done a little practising – I hadn't played an instrument in a long time – but some things you don't forget. Mike, Gabe, Peter and Paul were all dressed, made-up and tuning up (if the sounds coming up could be called tunes). Morgan, Chase and the rest of 'the girls' were downstairs taking care of final rehearsals; Ashe, Hel and Phoenix were doing their hair and makeup in MY bathroom, along with Jezebel, who had arrived a little while ago. If they dared to complain about having to wait for *me*.

I slipped on my boots and adjusted the lacing on my trousers. Bending wasn't going to be easy – and I might have to stand up all night, I thought. Still given the fact that the laces did give some degree of allowance (given the fact that I was laced from ankle to waist), I had to hope I wouldn't need the 'little boys' room'. I was also not sure whether the design leaving me unable to wear underwear was an advantage or not.

Finally, I was admitted to the bathroom. "You CAN leave, you know," I pointed out, sitting before the mirror.

"Oh, we're in no hurry," Jez laughed.

"Now you tell me!" I retorted.

"Oh, come on, boss, I've never seen you get ready for a performance," she giggled. I scowled, but they were clearly going nowhere so I tied back my hair and applied the white base to my face, before carefully painting on the black patterns and gelling my hair into spikes. When I was satisfied, I sat back and looked myself over. I would do. I rose and turned to face my audience.

"Well, ladies? Will I do?"

Hel handed me the vest, which I slipped on, and began lacing me up. "This is a novelty," she grinned, leaning towards me.

"Careful, don't strain his laces," Phoenix giggled.

"Oh, it might be interesting," Hel purred, running a nail down the exposed part of my chest.

"Okay, ladies," I laughed. "Enough is enough. Shall we go, before we forget where we are supposed to be?"

"Spoilsport!" they chorused.

We walked to the bar to find Ricky and Lucas, also in costume, tossing cocktail mixers and juggling in perfect time. "Make mine a 'Temptation'," I asked as the ladies dispersed.

"One 'Temptation' coming up," Lucas said, grinning broadly. I watched with a mixture of pride and unease as he prepared.

I looked at Ricky. "Er – you don't mind, do you, boss?" He gestured to Lucas.

"I guess not. As long as it's just preparation."

"I hear."

"One 'Temptation', Father." He looked at me, eager for my approval. I sipped. It was good. VERY GOOD. Silently, I extended my glass. His grin widened, and he poured.

By the time I hit the stage, the spirit was coursing through my blood (because I allowed it to, having convinced myself I needed its support). I thought of Jim Morrison and The Doors, and grinned. Showtime!

[I had half decided not to attend Luc's party, after our conversation . . . but I had promised my staff and did not wish to renege. There had been a time when we had been close, my brother and I . . . but I had not liked living in his shadow. Had Mother fuelled my ambition? Perhaps she had. I knew I could not BE Luc, but I did not want to be. I was the solid one, the reliable one, the less colourful one . . . I did not mind. However, listening to my staff discussing the physical attributes of my bizarrely dressed brother, I could not help being a little jealous!

He would tease me, no doubt, about raiding the place . . . but then, I'd probably have to arrest half of my own staff – and that would be more than a little embarrassing!

Actually, I could quite look forward to telling him what they wanted to do with/to him! It would be interesting to see his reaction.

Whatever you might think of his morals, Luc does have his own moral code, and I have seen him almost naively unaware of his own attractions. Oh, not always. There are times when Luc knows and intends what he does.

"Come on, boss, let your hair down," I heard.

"Let it all hang out!"

Personally, I thought Luc had enough flesh on display for both of us! Nevertheless, not wishing to be a killjoy, I headed for the dance floor. Luc grinned and leapt down from the stage.

"Nice outfit," I said.]

"Thanks. I rather like it myself."

"Not into body piercing?"

"No," I grinned. "Too squeamish."

"Yeah – right."

"Enjoy," I said, spreading my arms. "Drinks on the house. Cut loose, bro. At least for tonight."

"And tomorrow be damned?"

"Tomorrow never comes," I said in reply.

"Luc!" I glanced back towards the stage, where the guys were gesturing to me.

"Gotta go," I said, heading for the stage.

"Don't know about you," Gabe said as I leapt up, "but all this leather is making me sweat."

"Think of it as a slimming aid," I laughed, pulling a towel across my body.

"I don't need to slim!" he complained indignantly, as I adjusted the microphone.

"Course not," Mike chuckled. "Ready?"

I grimaced. "I guess." I looked out into the audience with a degree of unease. The atmosphere was hot and heavy – steamy – and I had a horrible feeling some bright spark had released pheromones into the atmosphere – or some hallucinogen. I gestured to one of my staff, whispered commands, which sent him scurrying to hit the room with an antidote, just in case. I didn't like the way the audience was looking at me – I was wearing little enough as it was without losing what was left! Fortunately, the atmosphere eased and we breathed a collective sigh of relief. I had no reason to believe it was malicious – just someone's sense of humour.

It was a wild night, but, as the saying goes, a good time was had by all – if the amount of clearing up afterwards was ought to go by!

I was getting a little concerned by my 'family's sudden urged to go shopping . . . and their apparent designs on my wardrobe!

" . . . But it was a bargain!" I heard Lucas say plaintively as I entered. Four guilty faces turned my way.

"Lu–cas?" I asked. "What have you done?"

"Spent a little too much," chuckled Phoenix.

"Oh. That's unusual?" I sighed. "Dare I ask on what?"

Lucas grinned. "Go ahead."

"On what?"

"Ha ha. Go on – open."

I glanced at their faces. Was I supposed to make some witty comment? They were ganging up on me – I could tell. Looking into Lucas's sparkling eyes, I sighed and began to open the large package. He was itching to help, positively twitching with anticipation. Lifting the lid, I pulled back the tissue and caught my breath. Inside was a white fur coat. A calf-length fur coat.

"It's not real," he hastened to point out. "Well it is – but not – I mean –"

"I know," I laughed. I recognised the label – Xavier's dealt in fur and leather – but it was 'artificial' in the sense that it was cloned. Sort of . . . and I do have a fondness for fur.

"Go on – try it on," he urged, knowing that once I had it on, I was hardly likely to bawl him out for spending too much. Besides, I had a pair of white leather trousers that would go just perfectly with it. Indulgently, I obeyed. It had a high collar, and deep pockets, and looked spectacular. The cut was superb, of course.

[Oh boy, I thought, looking at Luc. I knew Hel and Phoenix were thinking the same as I was – that it was not merely the coat that was spectacular but the person who wore it. The collar was a perfect frame for his hair, and seemed to set his eyes ablaze. Lucas had had an idea for a charity night, where we could all dress up and 'strut our stuff'

– I could just imagine Luc on the catwalk in that spectacular coat. He would play it up for all it was worth, of course. If half the partygoers had wanted to rip his clothes off, they'd be positively lusting after him then! I grinned. Perhaps we could have an auction . . . he'd raise a fortune!!]

There's a conspiracy going, I thought, looking at their faces, and I had a feeling it was going to be at my expense! I had a feeling it was something about which I didn't want to know. "Come on, folks – out. I'm sure we all have things to do . . ."

I did. I had a call to make. Dam had been sending me messages for an age – and I had been avoiding him. I'd had Jez lying through her teeth about my location. I did not want to respond to his call – I knew we would argue – but he was going to storm my office, I thought, if I did not. Talking of 'Storms', I thought, I'd been neglecting my Hellsteed. A few moments more, I thought, slipping out 'the back way'.

Storm was waiting for me, as if he had anticipated my coming. Perhaps he had. While we rode the desolately beautiful landscape, we could forget all but the moment, the wind of passage in mane and hair.

[I could see Luc's progression across the landscape by the flames coming from Storm's hooves. I had been tipped off that he had left The Inferno of course – and as I knew from experience where he liked to ride, it was not hard to place myself in his path, so to speak. I was taking a risk, I knew. Whatever Luc and I had shared in the past, however, it had shaped us. I knew that he was avoiding me for the very reason I was there at all. I had to try and bring this to a head before it poisoned us all beyond redemption – but how far was I prepared to go? I did not know.

I am not a fool – nor am I naive. I have my faults, as does Luc . . . but I respect him. There are a lot worse people who have ruled Hell – and who were waiting in the wings for him to fall.

Better the Devil you know, mmm?

I waited patiently for him to halt. He reined in Storm, hooves flashing close to my face. He looked down at me, flushed with exhilaration, his hair wild and windswept.

"Dam," he said in acknowledgement – or curse!

"You didn't answer my calls, bro."

He looked a little guilty as he dismounted, letting Storm go free, brushing back his hair.]

"Can you blame me?"

"Guess not," Dam smiled. "I guess in your shoes – or boots – I'd avoid me too."

I smiled. "Peacemaking again, Dam?"

"Someone has to. Can I say my piece, Luc?"

"Go ahead."

"And the Devil take the hindmost?" A smile flickered. "I'm not going to plead, Lu. I have my pride too . . . but if I thought it would help, I would go down on my knees."

He had not called me 'Lu' in a long time. It had been his childhood name for me. Was it deliberate? Probably. Adam may be a lot of things, but he's a politician of sorts, as I am. He's not above a little emotional blackmail either. Yet, I had to give him respect – he was willing to humble himself by coming to me, even if he was as calculating a bastard as I was. We shared the same mother, after all.

"She's been asking for you, Luc. She wants a chance to explain. Says she's come to her senses."

I considered for a few moments. "No, Dam. I don't think so. You know me – I'll lose my temper and say something I can't take back."

He snorted. "You can be a cold, calculating bastard if you have to be, and you know it."

I winced internally . . . too close for comfort, that one. "Not where she's concerned." I replied. "She set it up for me to kill my father! Our father!"

"I know," he sighed. "And I DO understand. Part of me says 'Let him do whatever he wants' . . . but part of me also says that is the worst thing I can do. There's been enough family blood spilled. One last try, Lu. Please. After that, if it will satisfy, I'll lock her up and throw away the key."

I looked into his eyes, and wished I hadn't. "You're a devious, manipulative bastard, Dam."

"Just like you," he grinned. "Would it help if I came with you? What she might try if you are alone might not be what she will try before a witness . . ."

"Okay. Let's get it over with."

"Now?"

"Before I change my mind."

Adam nodded. "But before we go on our little visit, I'd like to take you on a little detour." He was grinning like a schoolboy.

"Why not?" I responded, shrugging, glad of any excuse not to go just yet on a visit I did not want to make in the first place. He took me to his office and crossed to a side door, which he opened.

"You're not the only one who likes to play games and solve puzzles. Look who I've found." He stepped aside, grinning like a Cheshire cat.

I'm not often lost for words, as you can probably tell – but I shook my head as the object of his amusement was revealed. I looked in astonishment at the small, perfectly formed figure as she flew (literally!) into my arms, and squeaked "Pagan!" I crushed her to me.

"Let me go!" she laughed musically.

"But – how?"

"When I took over the seat, I took over the files. I simply revoked the exile."

I shook my head, aware that I had tears rolling down my face. Not caring. I think I am excused a little emotion – I hadn't seen my baby sister (well, half sister, I suppose), for a couple of millennia. (I should explain Pagan is about half my height, and a fully formed adult woman who has the most beautiful pair of gossamer wings, long white hair, and violet eyes – the result of a liaison between our father and a Sidhe [fairy, to you] woman.)

As I hugged her to me, wiping my eyes on her sleeve, I peered between her wings at my brother. "If you tell anyone, I'll have your balls!" I warned him.

He roared with laughter. "Sure you will. Don't worry, your macho image is safe with me."

"Adam tells me you have a son, Luc," Pagan said. "Is he with you?"

"He's in The Inferno with Hel, Phoenix and Ashe. You'll meet him soon, I'm sure."

"Soonest, if you're willing," Adam pointed out. "It could get nasty here, and I'd like you to be safe."

"And you can disclaim any knowledge of her whereabouts if asked," I said.

"Well, you're the Father of Lies, aren't you?" Dam chuckled. "Anyway, you're better at it than I am. You always were. I'll call down . . ."

"So – what do you know?" I asked Dam, as we made our way to 'visit' at last.

"I don't KNOW anything for sure." Adam glanced my way.

"But your intelligence service is dropping hints."

"Yeah – something like that. She has friends who want to break her out at the very least."

"And?"

"I want to know who."

"I bet you do!" I replied. I had a feeling that Dam wasn't telling me all of it, but he did not need to – I could make a guess. The question was what part did he want me to play? I had a nasty feeling I was going to play the bad guy again.

As we entered the complex where our mother was held, I hesitated for a moment in the garden outside, unwilling to enter the sterile staircase. I had little choice, however. I had reached the point of no return. We climbed the staircase together, side by side, and it was in this way we entered the room.

Gaia looked slowly towards the door as it closed behind us, and straightened. "I asked to speak with him alone," she said.

"No go, I'm afraid. It's either both of us or neither," I said. We pulled up a stool each and perched on it, our movements in synchrony. I smiled in acknowledgement, as did he.

"As you wish . . . but don't hold me to blame if you hear something you wish you had not." She shrugged, indifferent.

"I rather expect we WILL hear something we wish we had not," I murmured. "I do not have time to waste – say your piece."

"And be damned?" she queried. I shrugged, not caring to answer. "I wanted to speak with you alone to give you information – a card to play, if you will . . . if you would cast it away, should I care? There is a plot afoot to unseat Adam. Had I given you the information, it would have given you a step back."

"Two problems come to mind," I pointed out, glancing sideways at Adam. "One, Adam already knows of a plot, and two, I don't want to go back."

"Better to rule in Hell than serve in Heaven?" she asked sarcastically.

"Something like that," I shrugged.

"Then together – unite, and you could rule ALL!" She leaned forward earnestly.

"Mother, we already do!" Adam pointed out dryly.

"And without your help," I added.

Gaia snorted. "You think so?" Her laughter was mocking. Bitter. "Who do you think put you in power, Adam? Luc? Who do you think slaved and schemed to get you where you are?"

"All you ever did for me was kick me out," I pointed out. "And I don't think I ever thanked you for the only good thing you ever did for me."

"I gave birth to you!"

"And?"

"Do I not deserve some respect?"

I laughed. "Respect? Come, MOTHER. Use what brains you have left. What respect do you give us? Okay . . . you put us where we are. Perhaps. You do not keep us there. We do. We work – and work hard. What have you done, apart from give us headaches and a hell of a lot of mess to tidy up?"

"Maybe you should bill her for redecoration," Adam suggested.

"Nah, wouldn't help. It's done now . . . but he made an awful mess of the carpet, you know." I met her eyes. "That was a step too far, MOTHER. Uncalled for."

"They DO say that hell hath no fury like a woman scorned," observed Adam.

"So they do . . . but putting a geis on a guy for walking out on you – for sleeping around . . . come on, Mother, that's low even for you." I leaned forward slightly, looking her in the eye. "At the last, though – he was his own man. As he looked into my eyes, and asked me to let him die . . . to end it. His own man. He asked me to do it WITH LOVE." I saw her wince, and felt a smile touch my lips. I had a great desire to slide Slayer into HER heart . . . but words would do. For now. "So I looked into his eyes, Mother dear, as I slid Slayer into his heart. I put him out of his misery, Mother dear . . . and only Adam keeps me from doing the same to you."

I felt Adam's hand on mine and looked at him. "It's okay, Dam . . . I'm not going to give her the satisfaction. It's what she wants, you see. Martyrdom. I can see it in her eyes. If I kill her, now, in front of you – well, I'll have HER blood on my hands too . . . and I'll have broken the bond between us. Sorry, Mom . . . you'll have to find another fool."

I rose, inclined my head, and walked out. Adam was on my heels a moment later.

"Was that what you wanted?" I asked.

"Close enough," he smiled. He'd wanted me to say the words in front of her, and I'd done so. Whether I considered myself bound by them or not was up to me later. After all, I hadn't actually said I would not kill her later – only that I would not do so now. I had my suspicions that my dear brother was playing a devious game of my own. Hell, of course he was. Mind you, so was I!

I was on a prolonged visit downstairs when I received an e-mail from Ashe that she was going away for a while, which I took to mean she had a need to feed and was not going to try it on my turf. Phoenix and Lucas were also absent, and Hel was just about to go on a 'mission' for me, so I decided to get a little work done for a change (in Jez's words). Pagan came and went as was her will – she could not visit me down in Hell, because of her nature, and she claimed to be bored in Purgatory without me. I would have liked to pay her a visit myself, but without special dispensation (because of MY nature), I could not.

So I had to set my intelligence network busy with the little problem Adam had put before me. It soon came to light that it was more than at first met the eye. That assassination was the name of the game. Salome, my computer, tried various situations, all coming up with the same result. Not all, admittedly, blamed Gaia – but most did . . . and I knew – somewhere along the line – that she was to blame. I could feel her touch, her presence in the weaving of the threads.

Returning to Purgatory, where I tended to feel more 'at home', I could sit in my office with my feet on my desk without anyone telling me to take them down. Think in peace – and reflect on how quiet it was without the accustomed voices. I had been spoiled for company, I thought, and made the most of being able to spread out in my bed alone.

Okay, I admit it.

I missed my 'family'.

I was bored.

OKAY! (Tell anyone, and remember – the double glazing salesmen are waiting . . .)

There's an old Chinese saying you might know: Be careful what you wish for – you might just get it.

I was watching the customers from my balcony when they all strolled in: Hel, Lucas, Phoenix and Ashe. At least, I thought it was Lucas, being able to see only the lower half of his body under the pile of packages he carried. I watched them cross the floor, pausing to speak to various people, heard their laughter and considered myself lucky. And wondered what was going to go wrong. Or more precisely when. 'What' probably went without saying, as did 'who'?

I followed them into my apartment, wondering why they always chose to unload in mine rather than their own. When Phoenix poured me a drink and suggested I sit down, I began to worry.

"You have my attention, ladies."

Hel and Ashe looked at each other while I waited.

"They have something to tell you – and they're worried about what you're going to do."

"Lucas? What do they – you – whoever – THINK I'm going to do?"

Lucas glanced at his mother, then back at me. "How's it been, while we've been away? Quiet?"

"Too quiet," I admitted, puzzled. "Oh damn, what is it?" I asked. "Will someone tell me? I promise I won't be angry, I won't throw a tantrum, I won't throw fireballs, and I'll be very nice. Lucas?"

Lucas, looking very mature (how did he seem to grow every time he went away?), looked askance at Hel and Ashe, who nodded almost imperceptibly. "I don't exactly know how to tell you this – technically, it shouldn't be possible, but we've been to someone who knows about these things and, well, we're pregnant."

I think my mouth dropped open in shock. I certainly could not have looked my usual elegant self, because Lucas rushed to me with another drink. "What?" I croaked.

"Congratulations, Father . . . you're going to be a father, Father," he chuckled gleefully. "Twice. Well, you DID say you regretted not seeing me born, etc. Now you will. Isn't that nice?"

"Oh – shit!" I exclaimed, my eyes shifting from one to another. "When – how . . .?"

"Oh Lord, Dad, even I know that one!" Lucas snorted.

"LUCAS!"

He grinned at me – but he HAD given me time to collect my wits. Hel and Ashe were stood side by side, as if seeking comfort from each other – or protection from me. I took a deep breath. "Ladies – don't look like the condemned! Sit down!" They did. "Are you absolutely sure?" They nodded. "Hel?"

"We – I – yes. I'm sure. Phoenix arranged for me – us – to see someone." Hel would not be too much of a problem, though she was technically a demoness (well, half, on her mother's side) . . . but Ashe was a vampire.

"Ashe? How?"

"I don't know, dammit. I shouldn't be able to conceive! Must be something in the water or something."

"Or something!" Lucas spluttered. "You're *hot*, Dad!"

"Lu-cas!"

"It's true," he giggled. "Against all the odds, you managed to get two out of three up the spout at the same time!"

"LUCAS!" we all chorused, as he sat down heavily on the floor, laughing.

"Sorry," he hiccupped. "But it is funny."

Well, I suppose he had a point. "Er – how do YOU feel about it, ladies?"

"Okay, I guess," Hel responded hesitantly.

"Ashe?"

Ashe smiled faintly. "I was mad as hell – then I was scared that a baby might be born like me. The lady we saw says that the chance is only slight – it would have been different if I had been born a vampire, or something."

For some reason, that started Lucas giggling again. I suspected he'd been drinking. Either that, or there really WAS something in the water!

"But are you happy?"

She looked into my eyes, as if seeking something. She must have been satisfied, because she smiled. "Yes."

I shuddered inside, and smiled. "Good." I rose and opened my arms to them. "Phoenix? This involves you too."

She smiled. "You're going to need all the help you can get – and I've had a little practice. It's cool. I'm happy – for all of us."

"Then can you sober up your firstborn?"

She grinned. "Come on, Lucas." She led him out, smiling, leaving me with Hel and Ashe.

"Anything you need, ladies – just take care of yourselves."

"But what about you, Luc? Are **YOU** happy?"

I held Ashe at arm's length for a moment, knowing that only the truth would do. "Ladies, it was a shock. I'll admit that. You knew it would be – but how could you think I would be angry?

You know how I love Lucas – all of you. How could you look at me as if you expected –" I shook my head, looking from her to Hel. "I might not be the best of men, but I do care for you all . . . and I'll look after you. Is it that I didn't trust you, Hel?"

"Partly," she admitted. "You must admit it doesn't go with your image."

"F***k my image!" I said. "You've seen me with Lucas . . . and I WILL try, I promise. I'll change their nappies, whatever it takes . . . but I won't change overnight . . . can't change overnight. I've been a selfish bastard for too long," I grinned. "But I will do my best for you . . . and yes, if you need to hear the words, I am happy. Very happy."

I felt them relax into my embrace. There would be problems, I could see . . . not least of all because of the impending crisis with Adam. I would have a word with Michael, when I had the chance . . . and Spike and Jude. See that someone protected them and/or their babies, depending on what timescale was involved. Time flowed strangely here (hence Lucas's growth rate) . . . but, I reasoned, if I was going to have sleepless nights (okay, that's not an unusual occurrence!) so were they. Actually, as I've said before, I can survive without sleep . . . I had a feeling I was going to have to! I grinned happily. Contented. I wondered that those mortals who believed the myth of me would say if they saw me now!

Mike and Gabe were predictably amused when I told them the news, but joined in the redecorating with enthusiasm. If I heard one more comment, innuendo or joke, I swore they would regret it.

While this was happening, I was working on Adam's 'little problem'. I was concerned enough to suggest to Adam that he came to Purgatory for protection – but Adam, predictably, did not want to leave. He had to trust to his own people in some form, he said – not that he did not appreciate the offer. So I made a couple of calls – on Mike's recommendation – for the times when he was not there watching out for 'the boss'. Mo came highly recommended (Mordecai preferred to be called 'Kai', for some reason), as did Jed. (I can understand why Jed might prefer Jed to Jedediah. So would I.) I was reminded of the Latin phrase which translated roughly as 'Who will watch the watchers', you see. So I watched, and I waited.

There was an uneasy lull, a heavy atmosphere pervading that

made me restless. I could see its effects on Hel and Ashe, too. They were uncomfortable, even if Lucas was being solicitous. I could understand, even, them seeking each other's company over mine. What I could not understand was the weird and wonderful cravings . . . but I do not suppose I ever will!

Time dragged.

Finally, when I could take it no more, I called Dam. "Sorry, Luc. Dam's not responding," came Rafe's worried reply. My senses began to scream, then an image flashed into my brain – Dam lying in a pool of blood. I hit the alarm.

"Spike, Jude – Mike. Tool up. NOW! TO ME!" I was breaking all the rules, I knew. Consciously and unconsciously, I knew. I knew that I would pay later, should they ask a price . . . for walking in, fully armed, no matter how good the cause. So be it. Any blame, any penalty would be on my head, as it had been before. Mea culpa. Mea maxima culpa.

Almost before Rafe could respond, I was on him. He half rose, froze in shock, startled by the sight. I must have looked very different then – I change, I'm told, at times like this, becoming the image people see when they think of me. It's involuntary. I can't help it. I don't try. Perhaps it shields the 'human' part of me from the things I do at times like this. Without a word of protest, he released the doors to Dam's inner sanctum.

I found the fallen body of my brother in a pool of blood, as I had known I would. He was breathing – barely – his breath rattling in his chest, which bespoke a collapsed lung . . . his hand clawed towards me as I knelt at his side. He looked at me, and I could see myself reflected in his eyes. I recoiled, involuntarily, and felt his hand touch mine.

He smiled. "Never – did – listen – to my – big – brother – did – did –?"

"Ssh!" I whispered, caressing his head. "Mike? MIKE!"

"I'm here." Mike knelt at Dam's other side, giving him a quick examination with practiced skill. "You'll be okay, Dam . . . just get the bastards, Luc. Track the bastards, wherever they run . . . and the bitch."

I met his eyes – saw agony reflected there, and competence. I inclined my head, then threw it back and howled. My senses reached out, listening, smelling. I rose, grinned, and launched myself out of the window. I hit the ground at a run, unfeeling of the impact, knowing that before long, Spike and Jude would be on both my trail and theirs. I had my weapon, but I did not think I was going to need it. Why should I, when I had long, razor-sharp talons with which to rip out their guts, or their hearts.

I caught them, of course. They were not fast enough, could not run far enough, even with the Devil at their heels.

What did I do to them, you ask?

Are you sure you want to know?

The blood lust was on me then. Fury at what they had done – what SHE had done – to us, her sons.

I strung them from a tree, both of them . . . still living. Crucified them, in remembrance of Jayce – flayed them with my talons and garlanded them with their own guts. I'm told it took them a long time to die. I do not think that anyone was in a hurry to put them out of their misery . . . but I heard, some time later, that Michael eventually took pity on them (or on everyone else's sensibilities) and slit their throats.

They found me, I'm told, knelt at the foot of one of the three trees, wholly 'human' again, covered in blood. It was dried and matted in my hair and on my skin.

"Come on, Luc . . . it's done. Let's get you cleaned up. We can't take you to Adam like this – he's asking for you."

"Okay," I replied, making no move.

"Luc – come on . . . I can't lift you."

"Wimp," I mumbled.

Rafe looked askance at Michael. "Why don't you have a go?"

Mike chuckled. "Luc!" He knelt, lifting my bowed head. "Luc?" he repeated, very softly. "Come on, big guy. Dam's asking for you."

"I don't think I can," I sighed. "Give me a moment. Just a moment. Or give me a lift. Angels have wings, don't they? Hover."

"I'm not even going to try. I'm an Archangel, not a helicopter," Mike replied, heaving. I sighed, and somehow found my feet. "Let's find you a bathroom. You'll scare the poor bastard to death."

"It's okay, Mike . . . I remember where it is," I said, straightening, and heading into the place I had once called home. I did not mind them seeing me bloody, but I would not let them see me bowed. So I held myself proud, as the Prince of Darkness, the Lord of Hell, and somehow made it to the bathroom before I collapsed. I had forgotten how much transformations took out of me . . . but Mike had not. I heard him chuckle.

"Easy does it, old friend." He ran the bath, ordered Spike to take my feet, and the pair of them dumped me unceremoniously into the foaming water, fully clothed. "Rafe, have some clothes sent up for him will you? Then organise food. He'll be ravenous. Tell Dam I'm giving his brother a bath."

Rafe chuckled. "Will do, boss."

It was true, I vaguely thought . . . in Adam's absence, Mike was in charge. Martial law, or something.

It only took a few moments before I was myself again. Food helped, and drink. I had a raging thirst. However, when they led me to Adam I at least looked my usual self . . . albeit a little damp around the edges.

He was laid in bed, his chest strapped, looking a little pale but otherwise a whole lot better than the last time I had seen him. "Hi, bro," he said softly, extending a hand towards me.

I smiled and took his hand. "The ladies send their love – and Lucas, of course."

"Thank them . . . and for the flowers. Did I offer you congratulations, by the way?"

"I don't know." I could not remember.

"Consider it said. Also an apology."

"For what?"

"Taking this less seriously than you did. And thank you – for my life."

"Dam – you don't –"

"Ssh," he said. "I do. I know you don't want me to say the words . . ."

" . . . Then don't," I said, uncomfortable. "I know."

"Sure you do. But –"

"Damn it, Dam . . . what was I supposed to do? I'm fast running out of brothers. I can't afford to lose another one!" I met his eyes . . . read his love for me there. And his understanding.

"Oh well then . . . if that's all it was. S'cool."

"Yeah, it's cool. I'll leave you to rest."

"Oh Luc –" I half turned back. "LO-VE the coat."

I grinned. "Thanks. Present from Lucas."

He grinned. "I think you give that boy too much allowance."

I laughed. "You might well be right." I hugged my white fur

coat around me, waved, and left him to rest.

I was uncomfortable with thanks, and he knew it. He would consider it a debt, however . . . and I was not fool enough not to know that there might be a time when that was a useful thing to have tucked away for a rainy day. As I passed through the reception rooms, I noted that the window had been repaired, and the carpet was missing. I glanced at Rafe at this desk, nodding my acknowledgement, and was surprised when he rose to his feet and bowed: his way, I think, of showing respect and thanks. No matter what happened, I valued that.

From his 'sickbed', Adam set in motion the legal proceedings against our mother which were his way of dealing with things. I accepted that, even if I did not necessarily approve. If I did not approve of the outcome, I could always take action on my own at a later date – and would. I suppose I had to allow him his way, as he had allowed me mine. Fair's fair, after all.

Besides, I had more than enough to think about as it was. While Adam was holding court proceedings, I had two very pregnant ladies in labour. We were running about like idiots (you know, the whole water/towels bit you always hear about). I would have paced up and down if I could have done so – but I had to keep calm. There were enough people having hysterics without me adding to it.

It was some hours until I heard the terrible and wonderful sounds that heralded birth. Ashe was first, and the most cause for concern, being a vampire – but Phoenix had that all in hand. "Would you like to hold your daughter?" she asked, as Pagan, hovering, mopped my brow.

I must have looked alarmed, because she laughed. "Just support the end that's screaming, and watch out for the other – that kicks."

"I think I know that much," I replied, adjusting my hold so that I could look at my daughter. "She's beautiful," I told Ashe, who was looking concerned. "Even has her mother's hair!"

Ashe laughed. True enough, the baby's hair was white, and stuck up on top. "Do you accept her?"

"Of course I do!" I said, realising belatedly the formality of her question. "Yes, I accept my daughter. Welcome, little one. Have you chosen a name?"

"Not yet."

"No hurry," I said, laying the baby in her arms. "I think she needs you."

"And I think Hel needs you," she smiled.

Oh well, I thought. Here I go again. I arrived just in time to
see a furious, red-faced baby make its way into the world. "It's a
son," I informed Hel, raising him. "Welcome, my son . . . you are
so very welcome . . . and you have a sister waiting for you."

"And a brother!" insisted Lucas, from behind Hel. I blinked
. . . I had not realised he was there. I'm all for sex education, but
. . . I sighed. There wasn't much I could do about it now, was
there? And after all, he had been holding her hand and mopping
her brow when I had not been there. He looked almost as proud
as a father, I thought . . . but then, he had helped nurse them
through their pregnancies. I would have to think of some kind of
gift for HIM . . . with their help, of course.

"Go tell the customers, and wet the babies' heads . . . or
whatever," I told him. "Just – don't get drunk."

"As if I would," he retorted, grinning. "Can I arrange something
for the ladies? Is it allowed?"

"I think a little would be allowed," I heard the midwife say.

"Then go ahead . . . oh, and Lucas . . ." I gestured him to me,
lowering my voice for his ear alone. "And arrange for flowers."

"With pleasure . . . and congratulations, Dad."

"Thanks."

I joined him downstairs some time later. They needed sleep, but
I didn't. My head was buzzing – and I needed a drink. Badly.

Adam received my news while he was briefing his legal team.
(Yes, they have them up there too.) He sent his congratulations
– along with a request for my attendance. Official. I was a little
uneasy, however. I had, after all, caused more than a little mayhem
in their Domain. Dam assured me, however, that I was immune
from prosecution on that front. So I dressed carefully, bound back
my hair, and headed for the elevator. My first instinct had been
to dress for drama, but I had no wish to embarrass Adam on his
own turf. For me, I was positively understated. Black suit, black
shirt. Adam blinked as if in surprise as I sat next to him.

"You okay?" I whispered.

"Fine," he replied. "The ladies okay?"

"Great. Blooming."

He sighed. "I envy you, you know," he whispered.

"You do?"

"Yes." He smiled. "But one day . . ."

I nodded. "Yes, one day."

Then she entered. That she refused to acknowledge the legality of the proceedings came as no surprise. Nor the fact that she refused to acknowledge our presence – but she saw us, sitting side by side. That was all that mattered. Appearances. That was, after all, what it was all about.

A 'guilty' verdict was a foregone conclusion, of course. Treason. She was to be returned to her Tower to await sentencing. She paused, then, to look at us – but gave no word.

"If you fancy coming down for a drink –" I offered.

"I'd like that. I feel like getting drunk, Lu."

"You're welcome, you know that. I might even join you."

"Your ladies might object."

"Oh, I think they'll forgive us once. Especially if you arrive bearing gifts and flowers."

"I think I can do that," he grinned.

And he did.

Then we went down to the bar, and really tied one on!

Somewhere during the night, we made our plans. I do not know whether Adam was nearly as drunk as he pretended to be, but then neither was I . . . Perhaps there are times when one needs an excuse to say things that do not come easy when the facade of normality is in place. I chose to take him at his word.

All I had to do was wait for the furore to die down. For the sentence to be laid down. For people to at least pretend to forget . . .

"Where are you taking me?" Gaia asked dully, as I stood in The Tower, waiting for her to dress.

"Do you care?" I asked in return.

She looked at me. "No. How do *YOU* feel, Lucifer? You have won. Do you feel triumphant?"

Did I? "No. I don't know what I feel . . . except empty."

She nodded, falling silent. I gestured to the door. I had promised Adam I would not harm her. I would keep that promise, unless she left me with no alternative. There may still be those who might attempt to free her – and I would swot them as I would a fly if need be. She had played her game, made her moves to make our worlds to her vision – and lost. Brought us perilously close to war.

Given birth to us and raised us, all for a dream.

Well, it was not OUR dream.

I had promised that no harm would come to her, and it would not. (Provided she did not attempt to leave her 'prison'.) There would be no physical torture – not that – but there are other ways. Mental projections – images of what might have been, and what *was*. Our images, Jayce's, Dam's and mine, on her walls.

Oh, her prison was luxurious enough – it would have to be – for no other would ever go there. All her needs would be attended to through mechanical means. Robots, if you will.

I smiled, finally, as the desolate white landscape opened out to reveal the plain on which The Tower stood a slender, windowless needle shimmering under the glory of the aurora. I brought the vehicle in which we travelled to a halt and pressed the signal to open the concealed entrance, before getting out and opening her door. I had purposely given us some distance to walk.

"Take a last look, Mother. A last walk. Run, if you like – there's nowhere to go," I smiled. "You might even say I made a special Hell, just for you."

"Does Adam know?"

"About this? He knows."

"And approves?"

I laughed. "Oh, don't look to Dam for help – he won't cross me."

"He always was a weakling!" she sneered.

My eyes blazed with anger and I saw her flinch. "Adam is as strong as he needs to be. You chose the wrong opponent in me, MOTHER. You trained me too well." I smiled ironically.

"Bastard!"

"Bitch!" I laughed, spreading my arms wide. "Aren't we a pair? Welcome to your Domain. I wish you joy." Sweeping a bow, I gestured to the door and followed her up the long flight of stairs, to the room at the top. "All you need will be provided . . . look, there are even a collection of family images for you to look at."

She turned to me, pain in her eyes – and tears. I hardened my heart. I could not weaken.

"Do you want me to beg?" she asked, reaching deep for a last vestige of pride. I could almost admire her, then.

"No. No, I don't. Actually, I want you to die . . . but I'm sure you're going to live a long time just to spite me. Either way, I'll win. One day. I'll leave you now. I doubt we'll meet again."

"Lucifer –" I turned back. "I did love you. I do."

My face hardened as I thought of what that love had meant.

"Tough shit. Oh –" I paused, a hand on the door. "Should you wish an ending, there's a red button under the glass. It will be quick and painless . . . but do me one favour. Don't use it. For a LONG time."

I closed and sealed the upper door and descended the staircase, sealing the outer door. I paused before heading back to the warmth of my black Hummer. I pulled the collar of my beautiful coat high.

Game

Set

and

Match,

Mother,

ENDGAME

I thought as I walked.

AND

SMILED

The End (for now!)

Game on!

Greetings, gentle reader.

Welcome.

Allow me to bring you up to speed and up to date.

It was pandemonium in Purgatory. It's not easy bringing up a family, as many of you will know. Particularly when there is a profusion of willing helpers, all more than willing to offer help and/or advice.

Which is why I was out of The Inferno and walking the streets. Literally. It's nice to be alone at times. Well, that's not exactly true. I wasn't alone. I was out with Elvis. Out with The King. Where he goes, I follow – and when we walk, people give us a wide berth. When Elvis walks, he IS King. What he wants, he gets – and it's, "Thank you. Thank you very much."

Elvis, I should explain, is Spike's Hellhound (okay, he's part dragon on his mother's side), and he's one greedy puppy. Eats anything he can get his teeth into. At the last count, I think: boots (three), tires (two), number plates (one), cushions (assorted sizes – five), socks (four – all different), steaks (beef – four), chops (pork – six), sleeves (three), bras (two sequinned, one leather). You get the idea – oh yes, and one duck (rubber!).

How'd I get stuck with him? Heaven knows! (Not literally, in this case!) Someone had to.

Actually, I like Elvis. He looks mean, but he's more likely to lick you to death. Unfortunately, a lot of people don't know that. Or fortunately, depending on the 'people', of course.

When we returned inside, the girls were rehearsing a new routine. Elvis left my side to take up his place at the foot of the stage where 'Hell's Angels' (Morgan, Chase, Cass and Medea, in this case) were pole dancing. I could not blame the guy, sprawling there with his tongue hanging out. It was quite a routine.

Life was, at least for us, predictably normal. Until an old friend came to call.

Late one night, the alarm rang on my private elevator. I was curious. More than curious when I saw who was there.

I hadn't seen Daniel for a *long* time. Daniel is a sort of cousin of Michael's, and is Guardian of the Portal, which is an exile of sorts. The Portal is – well – a sort of transport terminal, which we use to travel time – and those who guard it rarely leave. It does something to you, they say – though I'm not exactly qualified to say *what*. Perhaps Daniel knew. Actually, it's highly likely that he did.

Daniel was very dignified in his robes of office as he entered. His hair was short and grey, his eyes blue. He did not appear to have changed at first glance. Yet, as I looked closer I saw that he had. His skin glowed (oh, not when you look directly at him, but when you look out of the corner of your eye, when you're not *quite* looking . . .)

I smiled and opened my arms. "Daniel!"

We embraced for a moment, before he drew away. As if my touch – my warmth – pained him.

"Luc. It's good to see you."

I gestured to a seat, which he took gratefully. Sighing.

"Can I get you something?" I asked. "A drink?"

"Coffee? I haven't had coffee for a long time. Not *good* coffee."

I grinned. "That I can do." I played the host, and then perched on the front of my desk facing him. He seemed to be drawing warmth from the drink in his hands. Perhaps he was. "How can I help you?"

"My time is drawing to an end. I'm becoming – thin – Luc." I understood. "I need you and Adam to find a replacement while I still have time to train them."

"Of course. We'll get right on it – and for what it's worth – I'm sorry."

"I know." He paused. Smiled. "But that's not it. Not all, anyway. Which brings me to the other reason I came. The reason I did not just, well, call . . . I'm concerned, Luc. People – certain people – have been using the Portal . . . sneaky-like. I'm worried . . ."

Then he proceeded to tell me why. Then so was I.

The question was, what to do about it. After having a word with Mike, we decided that as we had to do something, we might as well enjoy it – and it was as believable a diversion as we could

come up with. Provided our own people played up with the
subterfuge (and they would) . . .

They say the Devil has all the best music.
Well, I try.
Welcome to twenty-first-century Los Angeles (which some
people describe as 'Hell on Earth' – so maybe I wasn't so far
from home after all!).
The Band and I were playing some 'live' gigs (the pretext being
that the ladies were getting a little annoyed with me and that I
needed to recharge my batteries, so I accepted Mike's invitation
to join The Fallen in La-La land). I guess I come cheaper than
hiring a front man or something. I wasn't happy about playing
'front man' – but with a little stimulation I could do it . . . and in
LA anything is available for a price. Or, to put it another way, if
I were hunting for 'lost souls' it would be like taking candy from
a baby! So I went out there feeling like a fool . . . nothing new
there I suppose.

*[Luc's wrong, as it happens. Or not entirely telling the truth. He
knows exactly what the audience wants – and exactly how much he can
get away with. As he says, like it or not, sex sells . . . and Luc is a
Master Salesman – Mike.]*

Why LA? Well, it had seemed a good idea at the time. I'd have
preferred Hawaii myself – I know I can surf California, but for
big waves . . . I had my heart set on catching something rad, but
NO . . . Still, there was always later. The volcano's always hot,
the waves high . . .
To be honest, there was a little more to our 'escapade' than
was open to public perusal. Mike's intelligence network was still
sifting through the debris of Mother's activities/allies – and a
particularly nasty little rumour was circulating that there was a
renegade on the loose with a very strange commission – to set a
quake running on the major faults, with the resulting slippage of
the ring of fire. The devastation would be massive – and unless I
was going to get the blame, I could not see what she might hope
to achieve. But then, who said she had to have any reason other
than to piss me off?
There were some, after 'The Fall' who chose not to ally with
either 'side' – rogues, who served whoever paid best. Mercenaries.

'Laz' was one; Mordecai ('Kai') was another. The most dangerous pair, the most unpredictable. Trust Mother to pick the best.

But then, I had Mike on my side – and Mike, my Michael, was the best there ever was. If there were such things as traditional 'sides' any more. As Dam said, when I told him, "Just take what you need, whoever you need – we'll fight about who gets the credit afterwards. Just make sure you WIN."

This time, 'Mom', no one, nothing, would stand between us. When this was over, I'd be coming for you.

As I contemplated the skyline at dawn, I glanced at the map spread out on the balcony floor. Now, I have few objections to anyone flattening LA. I mean, come on!

But San Francisco – that's another story! As I looked out across the bay, I knew I knew I could not allow THAT crime. I LIKE San Francisco. It's INTERESTING.

I like the hills.

I like the bridge.

I like to sit under one of the giant sequoia across the bay and wonder what they've seen.

It has a personality. Which is more than I can say for soulless LA.

Three more nights in the city by the bay, then on to Lake Tahoe. Now, they say the volcano is dead, but we would see. There are ways to wake a sleeping giant.

If you're determined enough.

Or crazy enough . . .

. . . and they certainly qualified by most standards as one card short of a full deck.

So there we were, playing our hearts out and playing detective.

Still, it gave my leathers (and my Kiss outfit!) an excuse for an outing, I suppose.

Welcome, friends and fiends, back to the 'den of iniquity'.

While our 'Lord and Master' was away foiling the plans for world domination and/or destruction of my nutty grandmother, guess who was holding the fort? S'right. Me. Moi. Number one son.

So, there I was, sitting at the bar while Ricky fed Elvis titbits behind the bar. That's when he came up to me.

"Well, what do we have here? The cub . . . and no lion!"

[I saw Lucas's hand lift slightly as it rested on the bar. I smiled and continued ostensibly pouring drinks. In reality, I was priming Elvis. (He knows all the tricks. Spike's a GOOD trainer.) Lucas looked the image of his father, sitting at the bar . . . I had to give him that. Knocking off a year or two, of course. In fact, the black trousers and white shirt probably belong to his father. The leather jacket might possibly be his, though. His hair is almost as long as his father's, and just as wild . . . and if the cocky bastard trying for a showdown is thinking that Lucas is not his father . . . True. That Lucas is a child. True (technically). That Lucas did not know how to handle himself . . . BIG MISTAKE.

I placed a 'Venom' at his hand. A smile touched his lips as he sipped. I signalled Elvis, who strolled casually around to sit at Lucas's feet. Well, as casually as a ten-foot hellhound/dragon cross dragging a ten-foot tail behind him can stroll, anyway.]

"Need a little help, do we?" he smiled.

I slipped to my feet, touching Elvis on the head. He yawned, showing an impressive array of teeth. "If I wanted help, I just have to raise my hand . . . but don't worry – Elvis has eaten . . . though I'm sure he would go for seconds if you had balls."

"Big words," *he sneered.*

So I closed the distance between us. "Oh, I can do better. I learned good. Which you did not, apparently. You see, it's not a good idea to threaten someone on their own turf without backup – or an armoury. If you're waiting for your friends, I think you'll find that MY friends are entertaining them . . ." *I paused for effect.* "And if you care to look down, I think even you will recognise a knife when it's pointing at your balls. And I do know how to use it. I learned a few tricks from someone you might know. Goes by the name of Michael?" *I smiled as his eyebrows rose.* "So, if you don't want to be singing soprano in the choir, I'd beat a dignified retreat."

"I'd take his advice, if I were you."

He looked to his left – at the figure hovering innocently in a cross-legged position over the bar. "We'll meet again," *he said, seeking the last word.*

"Oh, I don't doubt it," *I murmured, as he turned. However, I almost spoiled things by laughing. My Aunt Pagan had stuck a sign on his back with 'Kick me' on it. I grinned, sat down, and accepted another 'Venom'.*

"Well? What do you think of this one?" *Ricky asked, as I sampled his latest creation. I had barely tasted the first one, which he had promised* me prior to this encounter. This time, I felt it all the way down to my toes as it burned its way past my throat, heading south.

"A load of old cobras, Ricky," I croaked hoarsely.

He grinned, satisfied.

"Nice one, kid," Pagan said, settling on the bar. I shrugged. "But don't get cocky."

"I know. Next time, he'll be better prepared."

"S'right." She glanced at Ricky, coughing delicately. "My good man, how about a drink for a lady?"

Ricky grinned. "I don't know. I don't often serve 'ladies'. What do 'ladies' drink?"

"You've got a point," she giggled. "What say you that we do a little experimenting? It's kind of quiet . . . and Elvis can always drink what we don't like."

Good point. Elvis will drink anything . . . usually without effect. I say USUALLY, because when you say that, it usually turns out not to be the case, right?

"Okay, boss?" Ricky enquired.

"Sounds good to me." I shrugged, turning to rest my arms on the bar. "Shall I just sit here with my mouth open, or is that a little undignified?"

"Just a little, nephew," she chuckled. "And if I get drunk, you can always pick me up and pour me into bed."

"Sure." I grinned at the thought of an inebriated fairy and a pickled hellhound – and decided it might be an interesting night after all. "Let's make it a competition, with a prize for the best creation?"

"What's the prize?" Ricky asked.

"Don't have the faintest idea, my friend . . . but I'm sure I can come up with something."

"Okay." Ricky rolled up his sleeves. "Let battle commence."

I THINK I put Aunt Pagan to bed okay. At least, I don't remember dropping her . . . and Ashe says I didn't wake Trinity or Joshua (my siblings), which has to be good, right? So, how come I don't remember getting undressed, or into bed? I certainly don't remember ending up there with Chase, Medea, Cass . . .

I groaned and tried to sit up. "Morning, boss."

"Huh?" I looked bleary-eyed at Medea.

"I said 'Morning, boss'."

"Oh. Morning. Is it?"

"I guess. Coffee?"

"I'd kill for coffee," I mumbled.

She chuckled and vacated the bed, joined almost instantly by the rest of the crew. I might have enjoyed the view, had my mother not chosen that moment to arrive!

"Really tied one on, huh?" *She sat on the edge of my bed.*

"Yeah. Oh Shit," *I lay back.*

"Morning, Phoenix," *they chorused, as they paraded through.*

"Mom – I didn't – at least, I don't think –"

She took pity on me, even if she did give the most un-motherly chuckle. "Don't worry, son. You were too drunk to get up to too much."

"Thanks a lot!"

"Better luck next time," *she sympathised, patting me on the cheek.*

By the time I dragged myself downstairs, the place was lively enough to make my head pound. Still, as I approached the bar, Ricky had a coffee and a stiff drink to follow waiting for me. I adjusted my dark glasses, perched on a stool, and sipped.

"Thanks."

"You're welcome."

"Anything I need to know?"

"Not really. Got help starting – behind the bar. New girl – the Infinity computer sent her while she's sorted. Name of Shiloh."

"Okay. Just for the bar?"

"Up to her – and you . . . but as far as I know."

"Okay." *I nodded and regretted it.*

"In fact, this looks like her now," *he said, nodding towards the doorway. I looked – and felt my heart skip a beat. She stood there, poised and uncertain, then straightened and walked across the floor towards us. Tall, long limbed, built like an athlete – hair the colour of a raven's wing down to her thighs – cheekbones to rival my father's – of Native American stock (but what tribe I neither knew or cared).*

"Enrique?" *she enquired.*

"Ricky," *he replied, extending a hand.* "And this is Lucas."

She smiled. "I am honoured. Peace be with you."

"And with you," *I replied.* "In my father's absence, welcome to Purgatory, and The Inferno. I hope you'll be happy here. Do you want to settle in, or get straight to work?"

"Work, please."

"Okay. Cass – will you sort Shiloh a room out back?" *I asked, as she passed.*

"Sure, boss."

"This is Cass – she'll introduce you around. Look after her for me, will you? Show her the ropes, that sort of thing . . .?"

"My pleasure, boss," replied Cass, smiling. "Welcome to the madhouse."

"Thanks," Shiloh replied as she slipped behind the bar. Ricky was showing her where things were kept.

"The boss has a hangover – anything you can create?" he asked.

Shiloh grinned. "A test, huh? O-kay."

He watched her work. I just watched HER. She could have given me poison, and I'd probably have drunk it. I don't know what she gave me, but my head cleared in a second.

"Do I get the job?" she asked.

"I thought you already had," I responded. "But you're definitely hired. Are you a Shaman?"

"Let's just say I know a few tricks," was her response.

"I bet you do," I murmured. At least, I hoped so!

As soon as I was free, I settled myself at Father's desk and had a little look-see at her file. Including why she was 'on hold'. It turned out to be an unusual case – a request, actually. Given her heritage, she had been destined to go upstairs . . . but she had taken certain steps to make sure she remained in transit, so to speak, until certain matters were settled. The computer didn't go into much detail, but I got the impression that a feud of some kind was involved . . . a vendetta. Ashe, I knew, would know only too well what that might mean. I assumed that she had a scalp or two she wanted to harvest, you might say. Okay with me, provided she didn't make too much mess.

The file spoke of Zuni, with Navajo and Anasazi in the background and hinted that the problem lay in the marriage department. Now, from what I knew, women inherited property, and had a right of refusal in any marriage contract. I assumed someone had taken – or rather NOT taken – no for an answer and tried the age-old revenge – rape. Either personally, or on behalf of a sister, perhaps – but I sensed a knife and blood – and a ritual, which had perhaps 'damned' her.

It was not until I returned to the dance floor that I saw her again, or had any chance to broach the subject. In the end, I had no need to – it broached itself.

She smiled as I seated myself so I could keep an eye on the goings-on on the floor and placed a drink within reach. As our fingers touched, I felt a shock pass through my arm sufficient to send a spasm, which knocked the drink over. Apologising profusely, she mopped up and made me another, as I flexed my numb fingers.

"Sorry, boss. No one warned me –"

"Why should they? Not everyone knows that I'm weird," I smiled in what I hoped was an engaging fashion.

"You're not weird!" she protested.

"I'm not?" I chuckled. "My mother's an angel, and my father's the Prince of Darkness. That's got to count as a little weird."

She glanced at me. Grinned. Conceded. "Okay. A LITTLE." I nodded, satisfied. "I've never felt it quite so strong before. Only in The People –" She bit a lip. "What – did you see?"

I hesitated – brought my mind into focus. "A girl – running through maize. Chased by men on horses. A fight. A knife. Blood." I drew a deep breath. "Laughter. They're drunk – or high. She –"

" . . . Took her own life rather than be defiled," she whispered. "I swore to make them pay. She never hurt anyone – my little sister. I – hunted them down, one by one. Spoke their names to the wind and the flame – but there is a price, no?"

"There is always a price," I murmured. "So – who remains?"

"Only one. His name – he has many names – but I am told you may know him. His name is Kai."

Oh yes, I knew him. Not personally. Not yet . . . but my father did. Only too well. It never rains but it pours, right? Exactly how this was all going to come together, I had no idea – but I knew I had to inform my father at the first opportunity.

"There may be a way for us to – help each other," I heard myself saying.

"Rick tells me that I can trust you," she said, with an honesty that hurt. "But I find it had to trust men. CAN I trust you?"

"I hope so," I replied. "Do you ride?"

"Ride what?"

"I have – my father has – a Hellsteed. If I can persuade Storm to carry us . . ."

"I'd love to," she admitted, smiling broadly. "Very much."

"Then all I have to do is beg, grovel and bribe."

"Just a normal day at the office?" she quipped.

I grinned. "You got it."

Before I left the city by the bay, I paid a courtesy visit to the local Nest on Ashe's behalf. I had noticed (or rather sensed) a couple of them in the audience, and half expected a visit from them (my being their technical Lord and Master, so to speak) – but as I was on *their* turf – they were probably arguing the protocol. (Which might explain why they had not formally visited ME . . . you get the idea? Good. I'm not sure I do. Too many late nights – or early mornings.)

It was a dark foggy night (there are lots of them to choose from, after all) – and I made my way down to the waterfront. I was dressed in black, of course – my long black coat, its collar turned high against the damp. I could sense them in the shadows, watching me. I paused under a street lamp, the light reflecting off the ring on my hand as I listened for their voices on the wind. Voices *you* would never hear, naturally. Unless you were about to die. Or were already dead, of course.

Finally, tired of leaning on lamp posts and feeling like a hooker under a red light, I broke the silence. "Greetings, Children. Let there be peace between us."

For a moment, nothing. Then the shadows stirred and four figures became visible. "We come in peace, Lord of Shadows. Our Master bid us come, and bids you welcome. If you would accept his hospitality –"

I offered my hand and one by one they knelt and kissed my ring. "Gladly."

"Then allow us to transport you, and be welcome."

I laughed softly. "Young one, I CAN transport myself."

"Oh, we know your power," he laughed. "It's just that the Master sent transport for you . . ."

O-kay, I thought. Show off, huh? Why not. "Then I would be churlish to refuse. Lead on."

They led me proudly to the 'gondola' moored at the bottom of the ladder. It had lamps, fore and aft, and was sumptuously lined with satin and velvet. Now, you might wonder at the wisdom of crossing the Golden Gate in such a 'flimsy' vessel, but allow me to assure you it was as smooth as, well, silk.

I stood at the prow, gazing forward – at The Rock, at Angel Island, gave a backward glance at my companions and saw the ironic humour in their eyes. Angel Island. Right! I rolled my eyes and chuckled in acknowledgement, and heard their understanding and recognition in return. I had to admit, a self-propelled gondola is something I hadn't tried before. I'm not usually over-fond of water. Except for surfing. The exception to the rule, right?

As we settled against the dock, my companions jumped ashore to assist me, escorting me formally up the narrow path and into the large, Gothic-style house at the top. I paused to admire the architecture, but sensed their eagerness to have me inside, so I did not linger.

There were a number of nightwalkers in the rooms and in the passages as we passed. I could feel their eyes on me, curious. Probing. Some knew who I was. Some did not . . . and the ones who did were not telling the ones who did not. Interesting. Or not. How did I know? I had a feeling it was going to be one of those nights.

As we entered the 'reception' room, the crowd parted for me. Respectful of their dignity, I inclined my head as I passed, heading for the chaise longue at the far end. I had not realised until I entered the room who I was facing . . . but I should have. Or someone at home should have told me. Ashe, for example . . . but then, Ashe often had her own agenda, and probably had a good reason for not telling me.

I smiled, a genuine smile of recognition and friendship. He was dressed in white, as always . . . very un-vampire-like, right? But then, he was not your common-or-garden vampire. Indeed, he was probably unique. Standing almost as tall as I, slender as a reed but as strong as steel, his skin as pale as alabaster, his hair (long as always) pale as ivory yet luminous, his eyes golden/bronze, his lips parted in a smile of welcome which barely showed his teeth – only one feature apart from his unusual eyes betraying his uniqueness . . . his ears. His ears, like those of my dear Pagan, betrayed his ancestry. My host was Sidhe – faerie.

"Greetings, my friend, and be welcome in these halls," he said, rising to his feet.

"Thank you – for the reception, and the transport. It was – interesting."

"Thought you'd like it." He studied me, and I sensed hesitation. It HAD been a long time. I was mindful of his dignity, and he of mine, and we both looked like idiots until I opened my arms to him. Laughing, we embraced – and any lingering tension in the hall vanished. As we sat, he raised a hand. "Refreshment?"

"A, AB, O . . . ?"

"Ha ha!" He grinned. "Moët & Chandon, actually. It will do?"

"Oh yes, it will do." I laughed. Champagne tended to make me sneeze – but I was not going to throw his hospitality in his face. "Ashe sends her regards, by the way. And a note." I dug into my pocked and handed it to him.

He opened it, read it. Looked at me. "Do you know what it says?"

"No. She did not tell me."

"Ah. Congratulations, by the way . . . family life seems to suit you."

I laughed. "It certainly livens up the old place. Is it private?" I gestured to the note.

"No." He handed it to me to read. The usual courtesies – and a request for assistance should I need it. "I'm not sure what she means, exactly . . . beyond the fact that it IS your city."

He snorted. "Oh, you have a pretty good idea, I think. I'm not a fool, Luc – and nor are you. Suppose you bring me up to speed, and I'll decide whether toes are being trod on, potentially or otherwise . . . mmm?"

I inclined my head in acknowledgement. "Pagan reminded me you were a meddler, just like me."

He grinned in agreement. "I'm glad she's back. How is . . ." He gave Pagan her full name, which caught me a little by surprise. Not because he knew it, of course he would – but that he would use it formally. What was he saying to me that perhaps he did not want his 'family' to understand?

I ought to explain that Sidhe have very long names. VERY long names. About as long as a name can be and remain pronounceable – though it is rarely used in full (usually beginning 'Pagan', or in his case, 'Gethin'). Was he saying that it was Sidhe business, not vampire, or that all were involved? Or that it was a family obligation, in that as Sidhe, he was related to my half-sister . . . and through her to me? That a 'family' bond made it – obligatory – willingly or otherwise? Yet, there was no unwillingness in his gaze.

"Fine. Looking after my firstborn . . . well, I'm not sure if 'looking after' is the right term to use," I grinned. "Lucas is – very like I was at his age."

"Ah." Gethin chuckled. "And you left him in charge . . .?"

"Sort of. Phoenix is there – his mother – Ashe, Pagan – Michael . . ."

"And you expect him to turn up here, eventually." A statement, not a question. Damned right I did!

"If things turn out as I fear, it's inevitable. Let me explain . . ."

I did, giving him his full, formal name. It was HIS turn to blink in surprise. I grinned at him. I have my sources, too!

Gethin considered for a few moments, his eyes scanning the

room – noting who was listening and who was not. Or rather, who appeared not to be listening and who really was. Politics never changes, right?

"Come with me." He rose elegantly and gestured behind him. I felt a tingle as I passed through the doorway. "Keeps away prying ears," he offered, by way of explanation, waving me to a seat. His 'office', I noted, was as 'out of character' as mine was. I smiled in acknowledgement. He understood and shrugged in a self-deprecating manner. "I never was much for – conforming."

"No – you weren't," I acknowledged. Sidhe in general had a tendency to be technophobes – all that metal and all. Gethin was a computer genius – the best I had ever met. Better than anyone I had. He was also gifted, like all Sidhe royalty, with considerable magical power. Have no doubt, my friends – Gethin was a very dangerous man.

"It never occurred to me – do your people know where you are? I wouldn't care for Mike or Gabe to appear on my doorstep with holy water and crosses . . ."

I chuckled at the images in my mind. "I left a message to say I was visiting an old friend – and not to worry if I stayed out late."

"And are you still my friend?" he asked softly.

"You named me so," I pointed out.

Gethin looked down for a moment. "So I did."

For a moment, just a moment – I saw beyond the mask of pride he – and most Sidhe – habitually wore. The loneliness there. I knew how that felt.

"I missed you, Luc," he said softly.

"You could have called."

"So could you."

"Or e-mailed me, if you preferred. *Www.lucifer@hell.org/ purgatory.*"

"I know," he admitted, a little awkwardly. "Now – about your little problem – how can I help?"

Okay, if that's how you want to play it. Fine. "You could use your skills – and contacts –"

He nodded, swung to his computers, and set his long, elegant fingers flying.

"There. As soon as I have a result, I'll be in touch. You're at the usual place?"

"You know me well."

"Transport is waiting for you. I do not mean to be abrupt
. . ."

" . . . But you want your people back before dawn," I concluded,
understanding. I rose, not wishing to make it more difficult for him.
Then I knew I wanted peace between us, an end to awkwardness.
Before we had disagreed, and pride had come between us . . .

I crossed to him swiftly, and before he could protest, took his
face in my hands and pressed my lips to his brow. "Peace, friend,"
I said in Sidhe, then swept from the room. I had my pride too,
it seemed.

I heard nothing through my computer, which was how I had
expected him to make contact. I had assumed he wanted time to
think before facing me again. However, I felt his presence in the
Concert Hall. Oh, not unshielded. Gethin is too exotic to appear
in public without a 'glamour' to protect him (a 'screen' which to
human eyes made him appear, well, human) – but I knew he was
there. Mischief got the better of me, I fear – and I overdid my
performance, just a bit.

"Cool it, you'll get us arrested!" Mike hissed in my ear. I knew
from his expression that he knew who was out there. I grinned
at him.

[*Oh yes, I knew who was out there. I knew his 'signature'. I just
hoped Luc knew how dangerous a game he was playing. A jealous Nest
is not a threat to Luc, not really – but if attacked Luc would react, then
there would be retaliation – and I really do not know the likely result
of a battle between Luc's power and Sidhe magic. I suspect that the
destruction might put 'Mommy dearest's little games to shame. Which
might just be what she wanted.*

Note to self – *point same out to Luc when he's in a reasonable
frame of mind. NOT when he's on this kind of high: looking at me,
grinning like a maniac. Eyes burning, stripped to the waist and still
bathed in sweat, hair lank – what you could loosely call a sexual magnet
. . . and every eye in the room on him. You could have cut the air with
a knife – and I wasn't prepared to be cut to ribbons if it got out of
hand. HE could deal with that himself. It was his problem, right? His
hormones/ pheromones/whatever running wild . . . right? Anyway, there
were always a few rejects lying around, broken hearted, waiting to be
consoled. Right? Ha ha – Mike.*]

I had just stepped out of the shower, having retreated to that sanctuary when I realised how dangerous a game I WAS playing, and was wrapping a towel about my waist when I realised I was not alone in the room. "Hello, Geth," I said, very softly.

"Just why does she hate you so much?" Gethin asked, over a drink in our hotel suite. I heard Mike chuckle and shot him a sour look.

"Choose any one of a hundred reasons," I answered a little bitterly. "For simply existing."

"Try simply saying 'No'," Mike offered finally. "It's as good a reason as any. Gaia never did like anyone to use it but her."

Gethin nodded thoughtfully. "I seem to recall something of that."

"As well you might." Mike accepted the plate Gabe, who was portioning out room service, offered him. "I seem to recall Gaia being responsible for your – ah – exile." I saw distress in Mike's eyes, an instant regret for something he wished he had not said.

Gethin, however, merely smiled wistfully. "Ah, Mike – Michael – do not grieve. It is a thousand years since Gaia refused that request of our Queen to allow me home."

"Would you go home, if you could?"

Gold eyes shimmered slightly – or perhaps it was the light. "To treat the path to The Grove again? To bend my knee at my Queen's feet once more? Oh yes. With all my heart." Grief was tangible in the air – and longing. "Oh, I know I cannot stay. I am – too changed. But to receive her blessing? Yes. Oh yes."

Mike looked at me, and I knew his mind. Could I do that – had I that influence, or will? I could try. "If a word will help – if I kneel before her –" I said softly. For me to set foot on HER land would require a great deal of grovelling, I thought, for if HE was anathema, what then was I?

"You'd do that – for me?" choked Gethin.

The air was hot and heavy, laden with meaning. "This honey-tongued son of a bitch will do anything he sets his mind to," Mike grinned laconically, stretching lazily. "Set tongues wagging in the Blessed Isle for a thousand years should he walk in there as a penitent – or as temptation itself? You bet your ass he would!" Laughter at least eased the air. "But to the present problem . . ."

"Ah yes," Gethin smiled. "The little matter of making California an island state. Kai and Laz are here – well, just a short distance away. San Luis Obispo, in fact. The Huntsman Inn, Rooms 213 and 214 to be exact. Registered under the names of Mr. Richter and Mr. Storm, if you can believe it. They have two drones at least with them, according to my source." Drivers/muscle men. "I do not know how much time we have – but they have a little gadget with them which would do very nicely if dropped at sea oh, a few miles offshore. A quake of approximately 9.3 would have a wave sufficient to put half of California – Silicon Valley – tra la, tra la, into the sea. Set off the San Andreas and Wolf Faults – and make what remains in dire need of a good ferry service. Is that of any use?"

"Oh yes," I said softly – but loudly enough for Mike, Gabe, Peter and Paul to hear and to gather close. At that moment, the computer link sprang to life. "Yes?"

"Greetings, Pops."

I rolled my eyes. "Lucas," I acknowledged. "What's new?"

He introduced me verbally to Shiloh, brought me online with events back home. The cogs in my brain moved. Did I need my son more at home, or by my side?

"Lucas – I need you."

I saw him tense, pride straightening his backbone. "Your will, Father?"

"I need you to use all your skills – and Pagan's help – to set up a dialogue with the Sidhe Queen. Set up a meeting, if she will, for my return. Beg – crawl – anything you must." He nodded. "I want you to set all barriers into force. All and every protection. I want the guard about her Tower doubled. Have Adam informed of this." He nodded. "I want you to give this information to your Shamaness . . ."

I knew I was putting someone my son cared about (or hoped to care about) in grave danger – but the stakes were high. I do not cast life away – any life – any more carelessly than Dam does. If souls come to me, it is willingly done – not on the whim of some crazy bitch! I have no need to set traps for people . . . people can be quite willing to serve me without any temptations from me.

"It will be done."

"This is your firstborn?" Gethin asked.

"It is so. Lucas."

"Lucas – this is Gethin. Give his regards to Ashe, and to Pagan."

"Pagan does not need a messenger." My half-sister's head appeared behind Lucas.

"Pagan has big ears – but she knows that," I retorted dryly.

"Of course I do, brother dear," she said. "I look in the mirror, occasionally. As should you. You look a mess."

"Flatterer," I laughed. "I've just come off stage."

"You look more like you've just got out of bed," she retorted, looking me in the eye – and over my shoulder.

"I greet you and wish you peace, Gethin*ap*Silvan*ad*Varesh-belCanto-Rel." My sister did not wish to be outdone, clearly.

Gethin's eyes brimmed blood-tears as he looked at perhaps the only Sidhe face he had looked on in a thousand years. "Greetings – and peace," he croaked. I lay a hand gently on the hand he had placed on my shoulder. I could feel the emotion emanating from his hand – drawing strength from me. Heat. Contact. Courage. Hope . . . whatever.

"Blessings on you, Gethin. I mean you no ill will – and will do my Lord Brother's will with all my heart. I am at your service, Lord Gethin. What little I can do, I will."

There was gratitude in my eyes, I knew, as they met my sister's . . . and understanding. After all, she had known an exile of her own, had she not?

"Your goodwill is all I ask," Gethin responded truthfully, withdrawing.

"You have it – freely given," she responded, withdrawing also.

"Then we have plans to make," I said.

"I'll set things in motion and come back to you, Father. Keep me up to date?"

"You know it. Ditto. Oh, and keep an eye on Shiloh. She's not one of ours – not yet. No risk."

"She is her own person, Father . . . she'll do as she wants." He grinned briefly. "But I understand. It will be so. Oh, I hope you don't mind, I introduced her to Storm."

"And?"

"She's true to her blood."

"Shiloh – or Storm?"

Lucas considered. "Both, I suppose. But I thought it might count for something."

"Oh, it does," I replied. More than he knew. If Storm would accept a stranger on her back, it said much – in more ways than my son could probably know. Hellsteeds are very clever. They have minds and wills of their own, and they know the worth of someone. It appeared that my Hellsteed had decided that this person I had not met would make a suitable mate for my son. It was a strange, unnerving thought. Well, I'd had stranger ones.

I turned to my audience, glanced at Gethin, who was curled up in a huge chair wrapped in his thoughts. "Mike, find Gethin somewhere to sleep . . . and transport, in case we have to move in daylight. My Hummer has shielded windows – ask Research if it is sufficient to protect him – if they will, bring it through. Make sure the team back home know what to do if there is a threat against Lucas or The Inferno."

Why was I saying this to MIKE? Mike regarded me with his usual laconic humour. I was babbling. Mike already had an array of weaponry laid out on the bed which would give any maid venturing through the doors a heart attack . . . but no one was likely to enter. Money buys privacy, right?

Mike knew his business, just as Spike & Co. did back home. Okay, so I was taking fatherhood a little too seriously. *I* think I'm allowed. If we were going 'hunting bear', I wanted to be armed and ready. For anything. Which is why I was not surprised when Slayer appeared a short time later, along with a note from Pagan saying that Lucas had 'opened a dialogue' with the faerie realm . . . and that my son appeared to have inherited my 'honeyed tongue'. I hoped she meant my gift of the gab. I wondered if I had done the right thing in opening my son to the influence of the Sidhe. He might find a few things interesting, however . . . but I was not sure whether his moral education would suffer. I had a feeling he did not need to absorb any of the Sidhe's views on sex. Still, he had lived in my house for a while – that ought to be some protection. Or not.

I grimaced. If you think MY morals are somewhat – suspect – you have not come face to face with anything like the Sidhe court! If I say, simply, that pretty much anything goes, and leave the rest to your imagination . . . ?

"Too late now," Mike grinned happily, having read Pagan's note over my shoulder. "You should have thought about that before you set him loose. He's not a virgin, you know!"

I raised a brow. Mike did not elaborate whether he meant sexually or diplomatically. I was not sure I wanted him to.

"He's your son, Luc. He's also his own man. Let him stand."

I sighed. "I know. Thanks."

"For what?"

"Reminding the Prince of Darkness that he puts his pants on one leg at a time, just like everyone else."

Mike laughed richly. "You're welcome. Anything else you want me to do?"

I considered. "You might see if Jude has any input. I know Spike is on it, but his Number One often has a slightly different way of looking at things – and that might help."

Mike nodded in affirmation. "What about having a word with Samael?" he offered.

Samael? I pursed my lips thoughtfully. Dam's 'Head of Dirty Tricks' had a fiendishly inventive mind.

"Greetings, Lord Lucifer. How can I assist?"

"I'm not sure," I admitted, smiling as I looked at the mayhem surrounding him. He was 'mobile', and the camera panned around as he moved. "But it looks like you might have *something*."

He grinned lopsidedly. "Oh, the Skunk Works usually does. Bounce my way."

I chuckled. Bouncing ideas off him was something I knew Dam did, and I had occasionally done so myself in the past. I was winging this one, which was not entirely unusual. I often worked better with my brain and my mouth in a different gear, so to speak. "I think a little diversionary tactics might be useful . . . do you have any trainees you want seasoning?"

"Always," he said, his gaze calculating. We often used newcomers in this way – not in any real danger, just a way of testing their usefulness. "Against who?"

"Laz, I think. Let my son and his little Shaman have Kai. Fair's fair."

"What do you require? Anything specific?"

"Oh, be as creative as you like. Just keep them apart for me."

"You have a day in mind, of course?"

"Of course," I replied, smiling. "And, if you give the matter a little thought, you'll know."

Samael's heavy-lidded gaze flickered. He was looking at Michael, who looked as puzzled as the rest of my wrecking-crew. "Give me a clue," he sighed.

I laughed softly. "Oh come on, Sammy." I did not say *I* had just twigged. A guy has to keep SOME mystique! "What better day for dear Gaia to set the world to chaos in my name, without anyone batting an eye? Samhain. All Hallows!"

Mike cursed and spun on his feet. I swung my chair lazily in his direction. "The thin-time . . . the time when passage between the realms is easiest. The one day when no matter how strange the creatures that walk the streets no one will question!"

I laughed, flowing to my feet. Mike was busy sorting his armoury, and I lay a hand gently on his to still him. I did not need 'ultimate soldier' going off half-cocked.

"Strange, however, that she should choose a day that marks the height of my power."

"Unless she wants to fail," said Michael softly. "Unless she wants to anger you enough . . . unless she wants to die."

"Then perhaps I might actually grant her wish," I replied lazily. "She bores me."

"Or," inserted Gabe quietly, "she is so sure of winning, so sure that whatever she is intending is beyond even YOUR power to prevent – well, maybe she just wants to royally rub your face in it," he concluded.

"I like the first version better." Samael ran a hand through his hair. "Do you know what she has?"

I told him what I knew.

"Hmm." He bit his lip thoughtfully. "I assume you're sending Mike and Gabe in to get the weapon itself, or is that for Peter and Paul? Mike and Gabe might be better at your back, in my opinion."

"Agreed." If Mike had not taught Peter and Paul all they needed to know, Hell would be freezing over sometime soon.

"I'd suggest a waterborne assault team . . . then, if something goes wrong, the water might at least cushion some of the effect. You could either disarm it, or use a Portal to snatch it and toss it somewhere safe. Daniel would probably jump at the chance of letting his replacement have a little on-the-job training. Thanks for that, by the way."

I nodded. "No problem. Herod rather likes strange machines."

"Well, he'll be at home at the Gate, then," remarked Samael. "I gather he's settling in just fine – Daniel says to tell you that he's seen few people with as delicate a touch."

"I'm glad it's working out," I replied. "If you think trans-Portal is the best way to go, it's fine with me. I don't want any repercussions, though. Tossing a bomb through a window can upset people."

He laughed. "Oh, I'm sure they'll be very careful where they toss it. Mike?"

"Yup?" Mike appeared at my shoulder.

"How does that sound?"

"In principle, okay." My team leader frowned. "Though we'd have to go disposal if it doesn't work . . . if you're unsure of your people . . .?"

"Oh, they'll do. I'll send Alexander with them. He'll keep them in line."

Mike nodded acceptance. Alexander was as good as they came. Not 'Michael', but good. If Michael had been 'mine', Alexander would have been number one on Dam's team. Why did I use Michael in preference to my own? Simple. I'm not a fool. I use the best tool for the job. Don't you?

"I'll leave the two of you to discuss tactics," I said, slipping out of my seat and gesturing to Mike to sit down. I had some thinking to do, and I did not relish doing it in my hotel room. I had a better place in mind. Had it not been daylight, I would have perched myself atop the Golden Gate Bridge to think. As it was, I headed for the parking lot, where my Hummer was parked. I joined the early morning traffic across the bridge, pulling up at the deserted panoramic viewpoint. At this time of day, the only occupants were the sea birds, and as I perched myself on the hood cross-legged, I let my thoughts free.

Please don't think me a 'goody-goody'. I'm not. I don't particularly care what you do with your lives. What a mess you make of things . . . but there is a natural order to things. A time and a place, if you like. As I said, I do not need to hunt for souls – there are souls enough in the gutters of some of your cities without my needing to go out and look for them: the drug-pushers, the pimps, the perverts, the murderers. But I do object to waste. You deserve your lives, just as any creature does. Time enough for passage in whatever direction when your span is done. You have madmen enough without our kind interfering.

Am I serious about putting an end to my mother? Too right I am! If I don't, she will not stop. She will do anything to get at me, and as you can see, she does not care who she takes out in the process. Call it a little surgical operation, if that helps. Or remember that she is not my mother any more. She is simply an insane woman who wears her face. Tell yourself that, if your conscience pricks you. I do.

I had not expected to be called to the Blessed Isle – but when the summons came, of course I obeyed. Pagan, I knew, was excited. Much as she enjoyed Purgatory, the Isle was her true home. She accompanied me on the swan-boat sent for me, and kept turning to me and grinning in anticipation. I had dressed carefully – not unlike my father, I supposed, but with my own slant. I had not wanted to hide my youth – almost anyone was young compared to the Sidhe Queen, of course – but did not want to appear totally inexperienced. My hair was short compared to my father's, so I had no need to tie it back . . . just a little wax. Pagan had told me that the Summer Isle was always warm, so I had chosen a V-necked t-shirt (Mighty Ducks) and cargo pants. Aunt Pagan said I 'looked nice', so I hoped I would do. Too late, if not. She could take me for what I was, as anyone must.

"Ready?" she asked, as the swan-boat came to rest.

"I do not know," I admitted, smiling as she stepped ashore and spread her wings. "But I am game."

"Good enough," she grinned, extending a hand to me. I placed my hand in hers and took that final step. As I did so, the swan-boat shimmered, changing form, and the swan glided gracefully from shore. A new cant on burning one's boats, I thought.

"Come, my boy," she said, pulling at my hand. I allowed her to draw me on, though it was hard not to stop at each new sight. I could hear laughter in the trees, wondered if it was wood nymphs or some other wonder – heard the sound of water and wanted to see if the waterfall fell into a pool inhabited by water nymphs . . . but I knew that I dare not step off the path. Not without her leave. I was alien to this place, as my father was – less so than he, being also my mother's son . . . but alien still.

When finally we came to the glade, I froze, catching my breath. In that place of rainbows, a unicorn at her back, sat the Faerie Queen. I tried to step forward, my breath frozen in my throat, but could not do so. I wondered if she was forbidding me, but something told me other. My aunt released my hand, leaving me to kneel before her Queen.

What should I do? I felt panic rising for an instant – wondered if it was some magic of this place, some testing. If so, I was not going to be found wanting. I was, after all, my father's son. Or, I thought, in this place my mother's! Sidhe lineage was matrilineal. Slowly, I bent my knee to the Sidhe Queen, lowering my head.

"I greet you, LucasapPhoenixadLucifero-diAngelus," she said, her voice musical to my ears, "and bid you welcome."

"*I bid you peace, Summer Lady, and greet you in the name of my father.*"

"*Not in your own name?*" *she asked, with musical laughter.* "*Raise your head, Son of Shadows.*"

How should I answer? "*I greet you in my own name, of course, Lady . . . But if matters are to be formal, then should I not do so in his name?*"

"*Of course you should,*" *she replied.* "*I was merely – being difficult, I suppose.*" *She laughed softly.* "*Leave us,*" *she commanded her entourage, gesturing me forward and to a seat close to her.* "*Do you wonder why I allow you here?*"

"*Of course.*"

"*Naturally you wonder. Partly because your dear aunt asked me to, of course . . . and partly because I was intrigued. I know little of the politics of your realm these days . . . I know less than I should, in truth . . . but time flows different here, and we do not concern ourselves as much as perhaps we should. There was a time when we cared much for the human world.*" *Her strange golden eyes met mine.* "*But as magic fades, so does out interest. Perhaps there is wrong there. Tell me, then, of how things are.*"

I wondered where to begin. I went back a little, to The Fall, and took it from there. She listened intently, her eyes never leaving my face.

"*Another reason why you are here, of course – were you wholly damned you could not set foot here – as your father could not. But he was one of the Light-born once – and as such, should he wish to come to the Summer Isle, I will not forbid him.*" *I felt my heart leap.* "*Tell me of him, your father. The man, not the Lord of Shadows.*"

Tricky, this one. "*What would you know?*"

"*What manner of man is he?*"

"*A good man, I think . . . a good father. He cares about those who come to him, those who serve him. He does not care to see hurt done without cause –*" *I laughed softly.* "*But he's no angel. He can be an arrogant, perverse son-of-a-bitch when he's of a mind. He can be cruel, but not without cause. I'm not selling him very well, am I?*"

The Lady smiled gently. "*On the contrary, child – you sell him as he is – with a son's love, but with faults and all. Had I wanted lies, I could have gone directly to the Father of Lies, could I not?*" *Her eyes sparkled with humour.* "*But even from him, I suspect I would hear what you have said. He is – human – with all its imperfections, and that is as it should be. Were he other, he would not suit his office as well as he does. Thank you.*"

"My Lady."

"I see questions in your eyes – ask them."

"About Gethin –" I hesitated. Should I use his full name?

"Gethin will do," she smiled. "Given names are well and good, but so longwinded."

"Gethin, then," I affirmed. "He is born of faerie – and yet he is a vampire. How can this be? How can two opposites exist so?"

She straightened, and I sensed old pain. "I do not know the answer, in truth. It is told that in your father's court the vampire nature is in abeyance?" I nodded. "So would it be were he to set foot there . . . but – I do not know the result should he set foot on the Blessed Isle. My advisors are seeking an answer – it may be that he cannot set foot here. It may be that his nature will not permit it. It may be that if he set foot here, his birth would assert itself and banish the vampire. As I know, I will inform you. Tell this, however, to the Lord your father and Gethin. If it is not possible for him to set foot here, I will find a way for him to receive my blessing until we CAN find a way. It may be that he can never come home to live, but if a way can be found –" Her voice faded away for a moment and she was lost in thought. "Perhaps it is not the answer you seek –"

"We are grateful that you receive us, and for any answer you would give," I responded. She smiled in satisfaction, a glance in my aunt's direction.

"He has been well trained, has he not?"

"In many ways, my Queen."

Mischief touched her lips. "Should I ask him, then, to feast with us?"

I lowered my eyes then, fighting laughter. I had heard stories of the Court . . . and was not sure I wanted to find out the truth.

"I have a feeling he might enjoy it," my aunt replied. "But I'm not sure whether my brother would appreciate the – ah – educational aspects."

Laughter bubbled. "Very well, my dear . . . I will defer – and extend the invitation to the young Lord when the time is more suited."

"Thank you, my Queen." Pagan almost breathed a sigh of relief, I thought.

"Yes, thank you," I added.

She sighed and reached out to touch my face. "A pity – I would have enjoyed . . ."

" . . . As would I, I trust," I concluded mischievously.

Her eyes sparkled and she laughed. "Oh, I do not doubt THAT.

Carriage awaits you, young Lord – are you staying or will you go, Pagan?"

"I will go. I feel a need to stand at his side until this is ended."

"Then go with my blessing. And you, my child." She passed a hand over my head, and I felt a tingle down to my toes.

"Is there – any message you would have me carry?" I asked, my voice hoarse. "To your son?"

She gasped, a hand touching her mouth, eyes wide. "How did –"

"As my lineage is written in my face, so is his, when one looks closely." I bit my lip. "Do I offend?"

"No . . . no." She smiled sadly. "Yes, Gethin is my son. My youngest. I should have – well – when he became – I should have severed contact, or taken his life by our arts . . . but I could not. Forgive me, but I could not. So I gave him exile . . . and wondered if it were not more cruel. So I cannot give blame to your father for his acts, when I have done as I have done." Her smile was sad. "I relented, long ago . . . and asked Gaia to allow him home . . . in the hope he could be healed. She refused – know you this?" I nodded. "For this alone I would give your father thanks – he has given my son love and friendship when I could not – even if they did have the odd argument." She sighed. "It is not all bliss here, by any means. We have our politics too. Perhaps it IS time for us to fade away, after all . . . but yes, you can send word to my son, if you will . . . tell him that he has his mother's love, if that is any solace – and that I have never forgotten him, or ceased to wish him well. Tell him that which I have said, if you would be so kind."

"Your will, Lady . . . and your leave." I bowed my head, rose, and backed from the glade. Pagan was waiting to escort me back along the path. I did not speak, nor did she seem to expect me to. Only when we were back within our own realm did I do so.

"Have Spike and Jude come to me – and ask Ashe to tool me up."

"You're going through?"

"I think I need to. I do not know why, but I think I need to. Has Father sent for Slayer?"

"Yes."

"Then – tell Shiloh we are moving – that if she wants to accompany me, she must be ready as soon as I receive the intelligence I need."

"As you will."

"Then ask Ashe to meet me in the office."

Pagan met my eyes, then nodded crisply.

Time for war, I thought. I was not my father, and not Michael – but I was good enough to guard Shiloh's back while she did – whatever

Shaman did. I had a sense of urgency, as I stood looking at the weapons cabinet.

"I'd suggest a short sword," came a voice at my ear. I grinned. I was not my father – Slayer was not my weapon. A short sword – that was different . . . or knives. "In fact, he left you this. For the time I thought you ready." She extended a box to me – leather covered, ancient, satin lined, holding a matched pair of fighting knives. Tooled, jewelled and balanced to perfection. I felt proud – and humbled.

"Thank you," I whispered.

"Come back in one piece – that's thanks enough," she replied gruffly. "And give 'em hell. You want me along?"

"No . . . no. I've a feeling we need to keep this tight. Look after things here. Whatever it takes."

She nodded.

I went to dress – like Father, I'm practical. Armoured leather jacket and trousers never come amiss. Won't stop everything . . . but prevent anything that you can't walk away from. Or hobble. Or crawl.

To everything there is a season, or so they say. Time, now, for revenge. Retribution. Surgical cleansing. Choose your own word, if it makes you feel better. Shiloh was with the second team – call it by whatever name you wish, but I wanted to go in first. I'd not destroy him, I'd promised her that – but I wanted him sufficiently weakened before I let her loose on him. Just in case. I knew how dangerous he was. I had Saul at my back, enough hardware to start a small war – yet I still felt the tingle of butterflies in my stomach. Scared? Damned right I was. Whatever else I am, I'm not a fool. I knew what I was facing – and that no matter how well I had been trained, he had a whole wealth of experience behind him that my whole team added together did not.

I was going to get hurt. I had no doubt of that . . . but I was prepared to take what punishment I had to if it would weaken him. Then, if she could not take him out, I would. Delay him. Prevent him from joining Laz. Anything I had to in my father's name.

I gave the signals, drew my knives. We were a strange motley crew, I thought wryly . . . but eminently suitable for this night. If the people of this town saw us abroad, they would mark it down to trick-or-treat and close their drapes. I hoped. I did not want them to see what crawled in the shadows. Not all I had brought with me walked upright on two legs. Or even had legs, come to think of it.

I do not know precisely how it started, other than in a blaze of light. They erupted from the motel, and it was war. The air sizzled and spat, *bones crushed and splintered, blood flew. There were more of them than we had anticipated, but it did not matter. There was extermination work to be done, and we were Rentokil.*

My armoured clothes took a number of slashes, but as I picked myself up off the floor I knew the worst was yet to come. I was covered in dust, bathed in sweat, my eyes wild and my hair – Michael Jackson's 'Thriller' comes to mind . . . but not only as regards my own appearance. I was looking into the face of – well – hell, I suppose. Lower case, naturally. I doubted even my father could have come up with a few of the creations I was looking at. My focus was not on them, however. My team could tidy up the trash. My focus, my only focus, was on the tall, lanky figure of Kai. Mordecai. Still with his Mohican haircut, I noted. A few more tattoos since the last time I had seen him, otherwise little different. Even in neutral Purgatory, he and Laz had been 'cold shouldered' enough to make them uncomfortable on their last visit, as I recalled. I had seen Mike talking to them . . . did not know what had been said, but perhaps I could guess. They had asked Mike to join them. Whether seriously or not, no one knew . . . except perhaps Michael, and he was not saying. The look on his face had been enough. I think that if he had been able to be both by my side and my father's, I would be fighting Michael now for the chance to face the formidable Mordecai.

So be it, I thought, straightening. Wounds heal. Pain is only pain.

I saluted him with the one blade I held, having sheathed the other. I could draw it if I needed to – but I was not sure how close I wanted to get to this man. Or even if knives were a good idea. He was very, very good. Still, there were only him and me; dust and blood.

"Very good, cub," he said, as my blade tore into his flesh. He gasped in surprise, as the runes flared. "Oh, very good."

I grinned savagely. The runes flared, rightly enough, but so did the wound I had inflicted on his belly . . . a mild spell, true – but enough to cause pain. (I took whatever help I could get.) I gasped in pain and rolled away from his leg. The blow had been glancing, but it was enough to give me pause. Winded, I crouched, blade in hand, my eyes never daring to leave him.

"You will not prevent us, little cub," he said, taunting. Laughing. "It's already set. Already running."

"Oh, I wonder about that," I replied, bored with his boasting. "Do you wonder why your boss is not here?"

"I don't have a –"

"Oh, my bitch of a grandmother might dispute that," I interrupted.

But I was referring to Laz. I think Michael, or my father, might have added to his scar collection by now. "Do you want to dance, Kai?"

He grinned savagely. "Oh yes, little boy. I DO!"

"Then dance!" I spun and lashed out with my foot, jumping at the same time so that my legs caught around his head as I leapt, bringing us down in a heap. I felt a sickening pain in my arm as he landed, and my knife flew from my fingers. We rolled free of each other, and I heard a voice I had not wanted to hear as a shadowy form came between us.

"Soul-taker, Oath-breaker, I call you!" Shiloh interposed herself between Kai and me. I knelt, holding my arm, knew it to be broken – retrieved my fallen knife all the same. I had two hands, after all.

"The boy is mine!" he roared.

Shiloh laughed. "Come take him, then, if you can. I am not my little sister. Pass me, if you can."

"I think not," said a voice, silky and seductive at his ear. He whirled to see my father at his back.

"Father –" I began.

He winked at me. "Don't sweat it, son – we all make a balls-up occasionally. It's allowed. Nice kick, though. Geth? Will you?"

"Surely."

I whirled, wondering how I had not sensed or seen the glory that was Gethin un-glamoured – but I did wonder what he was going to do. He smiled, and laid his hand on my arm. I felt the heat, then, and gasped. I saw his teeth flash as I pondered the weirdness of it – a vampire-healer?

"Please. Lord Lucifer –" Shiloh asked. No, begged.

"Oh, have no fear, child, he's yours." He still leaned nonchalantly on Slayer.

"Am I to believe you neutral?" Kai sneered, incredulous.

My father smiled. Not a smile you want to see, believe me. He shows his not-human face to few – but he did now – and his voice was terrible. "Oh no – but I honour the lady's right to call blood feud. I do respect that. Believe this, Mordecai . . . if she falls, I WILL take you down. Your soul will be mine, and all those you have taken will be free. You will be chained at my will, in full knowledge of your failure . . . and that your Mistress will not long survive your fall."

"You'd kill your MOTHER?" he gasped.

"As eagerly as she would have YOU kill ME," he replied. "But unlike that cowardly bitch, I do my own dirty work. So if I were you, I would pray that her power is enough to take you down. You do not want to know mine!"

This was my father's night of power, after all. Samhain. Bad choice, friend! I looked behind my father, at his guard. All nonchalant, all relaxed to the eye . . . but as keenly alert as he. He was stood feet slightly apart, leather clad legs braced, hands lightly resting on Slayer's hilt. Power glittered over its runed blade. Slayer was hungry, I thought.

"Have I your word that you will not interfere?" Mordecai asked my father.

"Better than that," he responded with a wave of his hand, murmuring softly. A circle of fire surrounded them. "As you will, daughter."

Outside the circle, the cleaning up operation had begun. I walked to my father's side. A faint breeze ruffled his hair and stirred his coat, or it could have been the flames – but the flames were not real. Or no more real than the images Shiloh was throwing to torment Kai. It is not a clean way to fight, to draw demons from the soul, every fear acknowledged or unacknowledged – but needs must when the Devil drives, right?

Michael spoke softly in my father's ear and I saw him nod. They were going to begin the other operation – or continue it while my father remained. I felt his hand on my shoulder. "Let her vent her fury, my son . . . cleanse her soul."

"How can this cleanse her soul?" I asked. "Surely it damns her further?"

"Not on this night. Never on THIS night," he explained gently, smiling. "Look – they go free."

And he spoke rightly – they did. Nebulous, almost too faint to see – but the souls of the trapped were going free in a column of gently glowing light. There was wonder on his face, and laughter. "This is the thin-time, my son. Passage to the Other Side is never easier than on this night . . . the souls of the dead come to comfort those they have left behind, and this night above any other those who are trapped can be set free. She does not damn her soul, Lucas. She cannot." He gave me a smile then, and raised Slayer to the sky. Runes flared, and the glow from the circle of fire flared in response, sliding up the blade towards the heavens. He had been Light-Bringer once, I thought – Son of Morning. Blessed above any other. If he was not those things any more, he could certainly be a guide towards the light.

Ponder the contradictions if you want to. I was too weary.

Suddenly, he tensed. I think he sensed her power weakening. That Kai was not broken beyond all hope. I would have screamed, had I been able to find my voice. Her head dipped, Kai moved – and Slayer leapt from my father's hand as if freed, seeking a home in flesh. It found it in Mordecai's belly.

The flames died as he stepped forward. He put a foot on Mordecai's body as he pulled Slayer free.

"Is he —" Shiloh began, leaning against me as I put my arm around her to support her.

"Oh no. Not yet." He smiled coldly. "I have a special 'Hell' set aside for him . . . He will beg for an ending, be sure of that. Or perhaps you might beg it for him, one day." He shrugged. "And who knows, I might even grant it. One day."

"You — broke your promise not to interfere," she said, very softly.

My father laughed gently. "No. If you think back, I never actually gave him a promise. Or you." His eyes held mine. "Take her back to Purgatory, Lucas. Have any injuries taken care of — Spike will know what needs to be done if Saul does not. Tidy up any lose ends here that have been missed. I have a little business yet to attend to."

"Do you need me, Father?" I asked, uncertain WHERE I wanted to be. He smiled.

"Yes, my son. I need you — but right now I think SHE needs you more."

With that, he turned and walked away, Slayer casually resting on his shoulder. He raised his free arm in a casual wave, and disappeared into the Portal.

"How do you feel?" I asked her.

"Empty," she replied. "So — what happens to me now?"

I was not certain, actually. "Well, the first thing I would suggest is a L-O-N-G bath. Then food. Then getting a little drunk."

"Alone?"

"Not necessarily," I said, bending my head to kiss her on the lips. "Shall we go?"

"But what happens after . . ."

I smiled. I knew what she meant — but I actually did not know what would happen next. Probably she would be given a choice — after all, as my father had said, she had not damned her soul. She had been in balance all along. The choice of where she went, or if she stayed, was up to her (and probably him!) — and I was going to use all my powers of persuasion to influence her choice.

"I usually wake up with a hangover," I said.

"Let's go play," said Michael.

Michael did love his work. Nothing wrong with that. Nothing at all.

"Lock'n'load?"

Mike grinned wolfishly. "Lock'n'load," he echoed.

Mike was always willing to embrace any weaponry, which came to hand – or terminology. I suppose I'm old fashioned. Oh, I do use what I have to, but I always have Slayer, and the power that comes with the job. The Office. Whatever. Mind you, if I find Mike walking around with a light-sabre saying "Luke, I am your father", I'll be seriously worried. Still, it gave me an idea for a theme-night.

"May the Force be with you," I said, coming to my feet. Mike rolled his eyes.

"Ready are we to go, young Jedi?"

"Come on, Yoda." I gestured to the team and we launched the boats. Crouched low, we moved silently across the water towards the boat, which held the device and Laz. Or if not Laz, he would hopefully be due to arrive. There would be company, of course, to be disposed of silently. Gabe was nothing if not efficient at waste disposal. In preparation, I tied back my hair and removed my long coat. Mike disapproved, of course – but I was not as vulnerable as I appeared. I have my secrets.

Once on board, we set about doing what had to be done. So Peter and Paul could look at that foul device and tell me they didn't have the faintest idea how to stop it.

The Portal it would have to be, then.

No other way.

I sighed and reached for my 'mobile'. "You locked on, Rod?"

"At your command."

I was tempted to say "Beam it up, Scotty", but I didn't. "It's all yours."

I was not sorry to see the filthy thing disappear – and not really interested as to where it ended up. Which was not necessarily a point in my favour. Bad pennies have a habit of turning back up, after all. Time, later, to amend that.

"So, what now?"

"The Sanitation Department take over," I replied.

"What about Laz?" Mike asked. "You're not letting him get away." A statement, I noted, not a question.

I stretched languourously. "Oh, I rather thought I might take an old friend hunting."

Mike smiled. "Good enough."

Mike knew, of course, that the person I was referring to was Gethin. I am sure that even Shiloh would agree that even her people were not in the same league as the Sidhe when it came to tracking. And Gethin was also a vampire. Let him hunt then, I thought . . . and feast, if he would. Before I invited him back to Purgatory, and if things went well, HOME. Yet, I could wonder as we moved silently through the great forest, whether the Isle would be home to Gethin again. The lives we lead change us, and sometimes memory and reality are not the same. I would be there for him, if that were the case – if he wished me to be.

When we came upon Laz in the forest where he was camped, it was as if he was expecting us. Or me, at least. Of course he was. He was sat by the campfire, not really hiding – his weapon untouched at his feet. His scarred face was impassive – his eyes barely flickered as we came to a halt.

"What, no smart words?" he said, finally.

"Have I need?" I frowned. "You knew we would come – that someone would come. That she would not protect you if you failed. You knew we were coming, so you fled. We followed. End of story."

"Oh, it's not over. Not yet. Not until she is dead."

"And you."

"My life is of no importance. It never was. Once she gets her claws into you –" he began, then stopped, looking up at me. "So you might deem it a blessing, a mercy even . . . but I doubt you are feeling magnanimous."

His eyes flickered to Gethin, then back to mine. Gethin was stood leaning against a tree, his arms folded, eyes half closed. Waiting.

"No last words?" I asked. "No pleading?"

"Is there any point?" he asked. I shook my head. "Then why should I waste my time or yours? I only have this to say – it wasn't personal. Just a job."

"Taking countless innocent lives is just a job?"

"Of course it is. It's done every day, by their kind. Why the – crusade?"

"What they do to themselves is by their choice – they have alternatives. I don't see the need to destroy just because she has a bad case of PMS."

"You don't get it, do you?"

I asked, "What don't I get?"

"Kill her, and you'll do what she wants."

"What SHE doesn't seem to get is that I don't care. I don't care to live with her peering over my shoulder all the time. Waiting, like a spider. Or a mantis. She doesn't care who she sacrifices, as long as she gets me. I do. I don't see why anyone else should suffer because she's pissed off with me just because I said 'No' to her. I should have taken her out the first time I had a chance . . . I'm sorry I didn't – but I'm going to put things to rights, as soon as I get around to it. Personally. Face to face. By my own hand. She isn't going anywhere. But I didn't come here to talk, and nor did you. You came here to die. If you want him, Gethin, he's all yours."

With that, I turned and walked away.

Gethin straightened, pushing himself fluidly away from the tree.

Silence.

Then, "Lucifero . . ." I froze, hearing Gethin whisper my name on the wind. Turned. He was stood, Laz hanging loosely on his arm, blood already drying. With the bond we shared, I could hear that Laz's heart still beat. "Forgive me." I returned to his side, questioning. "I cannot face her . . ."

I understood, then. How could he, with a fresh kill on his lips? I smiled and touched his face gently, a caress. "Better this way," I admitted. "Let him join Kai." I gestured with my hand.

"There's more," he began, stumbling. "I can read it in his blood. Oh ****!! . . ." I blinked in shock. Never have I heard one Sidhe-born curse. I had thought Michael inventive, being a soldier – but I've never heard *anything* like Gethin in full flow. I could not even begin to understand what he said. He gripped my arms urgently, pressed his brow to mine. Such contact is intimate in the extreme for his people. To share in such a way is a token of love – or despair.

I felt his thoughts tumble, my insides lurching sickeningly. Such was his pain that he spared me none of it. My shields crashed down and I roared in agony – but still he held on.

Perhaps it was because the walls were down, I do not know, but if time and space had ever held any meaning for me, it ceased in that moment. My throat raw, I spoke his name. Tried to sort the images in my mind into some degree of order. Horror washed over me in waves, and I'll admit that he held me while I threw up (– but don't you DARE tell anybody!)

"What do we do?" he asked, very softly.

"I do not know," I replied. "I really do NOT know." I shook my head, trying to clear it.

Smiling faintly, he brushed my hair from my face. "Forgive me?" he asked again.

A crooked smile touched my lips. "Ask me again when my guts settle down!" He chuckled. I raked my hair back from my face. "What do we know?"

"Not much," he admitted. "My knowledge of such things is – limited."

"I'm not exactly Stephen Hawking," I replied. "I don't know how she's doing it. Or even if she IS. It could be a coincidence. They track comets and asteroids. The Oort Cloud and the asteroid belt are full of them. Some are too small for them to spot until they are too close. An asteroid would only need to be a couple of hundred yards across to destroy LA . . ." I shrugged. "Okay, I know it's a cesspit, but really!"

Was she really powerful enough to create such mayhem? From what amounted to a prison cell? Yet I knew people throughout history had been doing just that. I had to work on the assumption that not only could she, she WAS. I had to leave no room for doubt. After all, I could.

The question was, could I stop it? The question was, what resources could I call on? Use what you must, I thought. Use anyone. AnyTHING. This is YOUR NIGHT, dammit. Why not see just what you CAN do, and let them explain it. Or not.

The germ of a plan formed in my mind. "I'd keep back, if I were you," I advised, shaking myself.

Gethin retreated, puzzled. I stood, legs braced, head tilted back, searching with my mind for my target. Nike, she was called. Victory . . . but mine, humanity's . . . not hers. Never hers. I slowed my breathing, drew power into myself, into Slayer's sky-pointing blade. I sought out a satellite, turned its eyes outwards. I could sense the panic as its 'masters' lost control and tried to find out how/why. They would have to explain why a 'harmless' satellite was nuclear-armed – but that was their problem, and incidental if they were seen as the saviours of mankind.

I felt the power flow through me, knew I had little time in which to act if I were to divert her or destroy her. Divert would do. I could live with that.

Gethin tells me I screamed as I let the power go. The pull from me was gut-wrenching as I gave the command to fire.

That I fell to my knees, unable to stand.

I knew nothing, of course.

Of the fact that he had taken me in his arms and brought me home to Purgatory.

Of the fact that even his healing power had been barely enough to hold me together.

Of the attempt to take over power, repelled with ease by Lucas, Mike, Spike, Jude, Ashe, Phoenix and Co.

Or of the fact that Elvis refused to leave the foot of my bed until I opened my eyes.

I knew none of this, until later.

"Hi, fella," I said, my voice barely recognisable. Elvis wagged his tail, rearranging my bedroom furniture. I didn't care. I stroked his big, ugly head affectionately. "You didn't eat all my clothes, did you?" He chuffed and shook his head.

I tried to rise, and sagged back gasping. "Oh – f***!" It took several attempts, but I made it in the end. Leaning on him, I made it to a robe and succeeded in putting it on. Eventually. Where were they all? Close by, I sensed. Why not with me when I woke? They had been, I knew . . . but I believed I knew why I was alone now. Ever mindful of my pride, they believed I would not want them to see me weak. Actually, I didn't give a shit. Pride comes before a fall, right? And the way my legs were wobbling, I was about to put it to the test.

I made it to the door by hanging onto Elvis.

The welcome I received as I opened the door almost undid me, however – and I was grateful for Lucas's arm about my waist supporting me. "Gethin's resting," he informed me, before I could ask. "He hasn't left your side. Well, hardly."

I understood. If he'd drained himself for me, he'd have had to feed. I nodded understanding – and gratitude for the steaming cup of coffee he placed at my hand.

"Just keep it coming," I said, sipping as they 'brought me up to speed' as if it were the nectar of the gods. To me, it was. Okay, so I have a weakness. Sue me.

" . . . But doesn't it hurt you – that they will never know what you did? That they curse your name when they should bless it?" asked Shiloh.

I laughed softly. That she should ask at all was a sign of her 'humanity' and how close she still was to it. "That's the way it IS. The way it should be. The agreed order of things, if you like. Anyway, it would ruin my image," I added, deadpan. She sat close to my son, I noted – hesitated almost to face me. As if I were judging her. We would have to talk, I thought. I needed to set her at ease – but at the moment the door opened and Gethin entered.

He looked pale, but then he always did. Dressed in ivory, his hair braided Sidhe-style, he came to me without concern that there were others in the room and knelt at my feet. I reached out to touch his hair and smiled. No need for words.

Respect cleared the room.

"Any word?" I asked.

A smile touched his lips. "I am told she has asked for me. And for you. I took the liberty of sending a reply – that by her grace, I would wait until you were strong enough and walk by your side." I did not belittle the gesture he had made by saying it was not necessary for him to wait. Gethin thought it was, his honour thought it was. So it was.

"Her response?"

His eyes sparkled. "She said that she would prefer that you were at full strength, but she would take what she could get – and that if you wished to make a journey to the Blessed Isle to heal, its arms would welcome you."

I took in a deep breath. Coming from the Sidhe Queen, that was quite an offer. "Tell her – tell her I am honoured, and humbled, by her words . . . but that I would at least like to *begin* the journey in a vertical position."

"I can guess her answer," he smiled. So could I. Playing word games necessitated knowing the rules of the game. "Your will."

"How do you feel?"

"I?" he smiled. "Well enough. It is strange to be here, and not hear voices in my mind." I nodded. "Ashe has been very kind to me. She offered me a wardrobe to sleep in, if I needed one." I laughed. Evidently he understood the joke, because he joined in. "But I was using a chair in your bedroom at the time, so I was sorted. Elvis snores, by the way."

"I know."

"So do you."

"I do not!" I laughed. He laughed with me. "Anything else I need to know?"

"I would have a word with your son's lady, if I were you. She is – afraid."

"Of what? Not of me?"

"Not of you as a man, but you as – well – master of her fate, I guess. She is afraid of beginning anything with your son, because she fears parting from him. It would be something of a long-distance relationship, after all." And I knew how that could be.

"A word to Adam, maybe?"

Well, my bro owed me a favour or two, I figured. "I'll have a word with her."

"Now?"

"No time like the present."

"Are you sure you're strong enough?"

I swore. "I'm sitting down, dammit! How strong must I be?"

"Alright, alright. Don't get your underwear in a tangle." He snorted, rising.

I didn't correct him. I didn't need to. "I'm not wearing any," I replied straight-faced. He rolled his eyes and departed.

A moment later, Shiloh entered. I saw her glance towards the closing door.

"Don't panic, child. I don't bite. Well, I do . . . sometimes." I smiled in what I hoped was a reassuring manner. "Take a seat. Elvis, move." Elvis obeyed for once. That was a good start. "So – how does it feel?"

"Feel?"

"Revenge."

"Empty," she replied.

I nodded. "Good. If you were gloating, I would be concerned. You are afraid, I gather. Tell me – what is your fear? That I will send you to 'Heaven', or to 'Hell'?"

She shuddered and raised her eyes to mine. "Lord Lucifer –"

"Don't be formal. Call me Luc," I said.

"Luc –"

She was panicking, I knew.

"Child, don't fear me. You have no need. Why do you think I asked you here, now?" She shook her head. "You don't have to fear my Office. If I wanted to scare you, believe me, I could. Should I need to. You know a little of what I can do . . . but I don't actually do it unless I have to. I don't scare people for fun. Well, sometimes it can be fun . . ." I managed to get something almost a smile. Good start. "You are not helpless, you know. You have skills . . . useful skills. I don't throw away useful tools. Whatever you are to my son, or may be, is his affair and yours. Not mine. He is old enough to make his own choices. You fear I will send you from him, I assume? Are you such a threat to his morals?" Her eyes widened, startled. "If you want to jump his bones, feel free. Just –".

I wasn't going about this very well, I thought. My brains must be scrambled. I took a deep breath. "Your soul is in balance, as it always was. You don't NEED to go anywhere, unless you choose to do so. You can stay here, in Purgatory, in BALANCE, as long as you like. I will even have a word with Dam if you wish, get it made official. Extended leave, so to speak. Does that help?"

"Yes, Lord – Luc." She let out a deep breath. "Are you feeling yourself yet? I was told to ask you, because there are several of your ladies beating down the doors . . ."

Relief brought mischief to the fore, and I grinned appreciatively. She was feeling surer of herself, and that was good.

"I'm not sure I know how to answer that," I admitted. The possibilities, which might flow from whatever I said, might be more than I could handle.

"Then shall I say you need to rest and . . . gather your energies?" she offered. "I could order you food – what would you like?"

"Ask Saul to prepare something. He knows what I like." When he wasn't acting muscle, Saul was the best chef I knew. "And ask Ricky to send me a restorative – or prepare something yourself."

She laughed. "At your command."

I could run my office from my bed for a few days, I thought . . . then I really would have to pay a visit to Elisande's Court . . . I had a feeling I was going to need all my strength.

I made it back to bed, knowing I ought to take a bath. Still, I thought, when you have a group of willing nurses, there was always a bed bath . . . and that could be fun. If I didn't mind a few wet sheets . . .

I suppose that even with all the negotiating I had never actually expected to see my father set foot on one of the Lady's swan-boats heading for the Blessed Isle. He was wearing his customary black, of course: black trousers, long black robe. Simple, for him. His hair was loose, blowing in a breeze, which stirred nothing else. I could not see his face, but I doubted I would see humility there. My father's face was not given to humility. Even now, I was not certain beyond doubt that she would permit him to set foot ashore. If he had similar doubts, he did not voice them, nor would he give any sign. Had she not accepted his presence, I thought, surely she would not have invited him. Him and Gethin both.

My father looked pale when he stepped onto the boat. There was a frailty, almost, about him. As if he had a wound not fully healed. As if he had given more of himself than he had anticipated, when he had given humankind another chance.

As 'Ambassador', I led the way along the path to the Queen's Court, preceding both Gethin and my father. It felt strange, as did introducing them formally to the Court, speaking both their names in full Sidhe-style – but it enabled me to step to one side and observe. To see Gethin's face as he knelt to receive her blessing; to see her face as she welcomed him even temporarily home; to see my father's face as he bent his knee to her. I felt his pain, then, and must have moved towards him because the Lady put out a hand to stop me.

"The Lord of Shadows is grateful but needs not take of your strength, young Lord," she said to me, smiling gently. "All that he needs, he will find here."

"Deal gently with him, Lady," I asked.

She laughed musically. "Do not take all the fun out of life, my child."

"Don't I get a say?" my father enquired plaintively.

"NO," we three chorused. And laughed. Joined by Father, thankfully.

So I left them there and returned to Purgatory, to The Inferno, to hold the fort. Just in case any of those who had tried to take over before tried again. In the unlikely event we had left anyone in enough pieces to MAKE a takeover, of course. Which was unlikely.

So I sat in my father's office, my feet up on his desk, and felt the loneliness wash over me.

"Welcome to manhood, my son." I felt my mother's arms enfold me, her kiss on my hair. I smiled.

"Yeah, right. Mom . . .?"

"Mmm?"

"I thought about arranging a party for his return."

"Okay. Do you have a theme in mind?" she asked, coming to perch on the corner of the desk.

"Sci-fi – fantasy . . . Star Wars. Alien. That sort of thing."

"Go ahead. Use whatever resources you need."

"You like the idea?"

"I think it's a great idea. We need a little fun – been W-A-Y too serious of late."

"How much time do I have?"

"However much you need," she replied, brushing back my hair tentatively. "Time flows different there, remember. We only have to send word. Lucas . . ."

"Yes, Mom?"

"Have I ever said how proud I am of you? How proud we both are of you?"

I shook my head. "I don't know."

"But you knew it – right? Your father loves you very much. Never doubt that. He'd move – well – Heaven and earth – for you if he must. So would I, if I could. The difference of course being HE can," she smiled. "And he is proud of you. Very proud. Otherwise, he would not trust you as he does. I just wanted you to know. Wanted to say it, I suppose. If he gets a little too involved with the little ones . . ."

Suddenly, I understood and laughed. "Oh Mother! I'm not jealous. I love Trinity and Joshua. Hel and Ashe know that. So do you. So does Father. You'll be thinking I'm jealous of you next – of Gethin."

She sighed. "I know. I just felt it needed to be said. SO . . . where do we start . . .?

You wonder what occurred on the Blessed Isle, the Summer Isle, perhaps? Of course you do . . . but I shall not tell. Not yet. There are some mysteries that should not be probed, some secrets which should remain unspoken. Suffice it to say that no one comes away from such an experience unchanged, though it is not always immediately obvious what those changes are. It is a place out of time, and as such exists by its own rules. Perhaps with time it will cease to exist, or pass beyond reach of all but its own. I hope not. We all need some wonder in our lives.

What of Gethin, you ask? Gethin is still as he was – the changes run too deep for easy healing. Perhaps one day he will be free. I do not know. I only know that, although he is free to visit the Isle he cannot stay. He is too different, and cannot wholly be at peace. The feelings are mutual, as is the agreement made. So he would come to Purgatory for a while at least.

They were planning a 'surprise' party for me, Phoenix told me – but the surprise would not be on me but on Lucas. Friday the 13th would be his birthday – and this would be his 'coming-of-age'. Well deserved – I was *very* proud of my firstborn. Phoenix actually suggested I go 'in drag' as Princes Leia. It might have been fun. If I could bring myself to cover my tattoos. You know about the snake – did I mention I had a beautiful dragon across my back? I don't think I have. No one had seen it yet. Except Gethin, of course. He was with me on that wild, WILD night.

Legends abound of the night the Wild Hunt rides, but none do justice to the cruelty and the beauty. One day, perhaps – one day I might put into words that night.

But not now.

Elisande gave me a parting gift – a red casket that she told me to carry with care. I was not quite certain about it – it sort of hummed whenever I held it – but one doesn't reject a gift given by the Summer Queen, and Gethin seemed pleased and amused by the gift so I carried it with care as she had asked. I did note, however, that whenever I held it, besides it humming, the tattoo on my back tingled. I gave my farewells, as mindful of her many titles as she was of mine . . . formal. We had said our private farewells, the farewell of friends, out of public eye.

I set the casket on my desk in my office on our return (the back way, so as not to alert Lucas) and went into my bedroom to find my costume. There was a sudden crash in my office and the aroma of burning, then the alarms went off.

"What the –" I began, standing in the doorway with my mouth open.

It sat there amidst the ruin of my desk, its eyes whirling in happiness/fear/hunger, puffing smoke from its tiny nostrils and chirruping. I shot an exasperated look in Gethin's direction. "You might have told me! What do I do?"

"Talk to it," he suggested, laughter in his voice.

Great, I thought. "Come to me, little one." I extended a hand. Perhaps it reacted to my scent, I don't know . . . or perhaps it had been imprinted in some way, but as soon as I was close enough, it launched itself at me. There I was, a dragon on my back and one attached to my chest, its wings half-wrapped around my neck.

"Gethin! Help!"

Gethin was holding his side. He was weeping with laughter, damn him!

"Easy, little one –"

But the more he tried to free me, the harder my decoration gripped on.

"Er –" Mike began from the doorway. "Luc?"

"What?" I croaked.

"I think you need the decorators again." He killed the alarms, thankfully. The hold on my throat eased a little. The poor thing had been half scared to death!

I snorted. "Tell me something I don't know."

"You've got a dragon on your chest?" he offered, giggling. Mike? Giggling? Great! Ricky had been inventing again.

"Ha ha. Whatever you're drinking, get me one will you?"

"Easy," he said, thrusting a bottle in my hand. "Er – is it house trained?"

"Does it bloody well look like it?" I asked, cursing as Elvis rushed in and my new addition launched itself onto the ceiling light fitting. It took an age to get it down, and persuade it that Elvis wasn't going to eat it for a snack. (And persuade ELVIS that he wasn't going to eat it for a snack!)

Mike was dressed as a wizard, his hat somewhat askew . . . and it looked like my 'Conan the Barbarian' costume was about to become 'Pern', given the fact that even if I could not ride my dragon, he appeared to be trying to ride me. He. Definitely a He, I thought, looking into his eyes. He was red, with golden spines and gold flecks on his scales . . . and he was going to be a beauty. But what on earth – Heaven – Hell – was I going to do with a dragon? The same as I did with Elvis, I supposed, or a Hellsteed. Find a home for it.

"Gethin . . ."

"Yes, Luc?"

"How do you name a dragon?"

He smiled and tickled it under its chin. It crooned appreciatively as his hand moved to the ridges over its eyes. "Ah, you like that . . . I rather think they tell you. Or you dream it or something. Shiloh might be able to help. I've not had the experience. You are fortunate – believe me."

What was The Lady's reason for giving me such a treasure, I wondered. Such a gift was not without reason – or price. Time, later, for that. Right now, I had a party to go to . . . and a new dancing partner. Sitting perched on my shoulder, it surveyed the room as if born to it as we descended.

Lucas came towards me. "So, that's what all the commotion

was upstairs. Welcome home, Father."

I embraced him, with more than a little difficulty. "Thanks. It's good to be home. Spike – can you find something for him to eat?" I turned my head as far as I could.

Spike grinned. "Something raw and bloody, I suppose. I'm sure Elvis will share."

"Thanks." I caught sight of Phoenix in the distance, and turned Lucas in her direction. "But this party isn't for me, my son . . . it's for you. Happy Coming-of-Age, Lucas."

His look of surprise was all I could have hoped for, even the half-spoken curse on his lips . . . but he was stunned to silence as I led him to the door where Phoenix waited. Her face was lit with a brilliant smile as she opened the door for him, extending a set of keys to him.

"Happy birthday, Lucas."

He gaped at the red StingRay and shook his head in wonder. Phoenix had tears in her eyes when she embraced him. As he turned to me, he hesitated, eyeing my ornament uneasily. I shrugged and opened my arms to him. "I knew you wanted one. She's old, but she's hot. Take care of her."

"Oh I will! Thanks, Dad."

"And if you need something a little more – aggressive – you'll find a H2 parked next to my Hummer. Just in case. Now, come on. Let's party!"

Even by our standards, the inhabitants of The Inferno were somewhat exotic. All manner of creatures both real and imaginary, characters from book or film, ghosties and ghoulies and things that go 'bump in the night', so to speak. Mike's wizard's hat was somewhat askew – Peter and Paul were centaur and unicorn respectively (which would make matters decidedly interesting if The Fallen elected to perform); robots vied with werewolves, zombies with fairies – all par for the course, come to think of it.

My father, of course, had a little unplanned decoration periodically attached to what little of a costume he was wearing. A decoration which left his shoulder only to delicately pounce on the titbits Spike tossed his way. I was helping Gabe with the music (a yeti costume is not conducive to delicate switches and buttons). Ashe, Hel and Medea were Amazons; Mom was Ripley (Alien), Ricky couldn't find mixing drinks in a Terminator exoskeleton easy . . . I hadn't seen Gethin yet, so I didn't know what he was wearing – or even if he was here.

Typical of my father to turn around a surprise party for HIM. Not that I was objecting, believe me. Just making a point. I was still not entirely sure he was back to normal . . . .or what passes for normal . . . but he was not likely to show or admit weakness. Hence, I think, his style of dress (or lack thereof). With that much flesh on display, people were bound to see the 'obvious'.

Still, any games my father might have been playing faded almost to insignificance as The Inferno's doors opened and Gethin entered. He wasn't in costume, but then, unglamoured, he did not need to be. However, he was not alone. He was accompanied by Elisande, her consort/companion, and the Inner Circle of the Sidhe Court!

To say one could have heard a pin drop would be an understatement. Or that the only sound was the sound of jaws dropping open in amazement. Her smile indicated the effect was what she wanted. Of course it was! Laughter creased her eyes – which settled on me as I made my way to greet her.

"Welcome, Lady, welcome All – to The Inferno."

"Our thanks, young Lord," she smiled. "We trust our arrival will not inconvenience you – do you throw out . . ." She looked to Gethin as if searching for a word, ". . . gatecrashers?"

I considered briefly the effects of trying to throw her out on her rear – fortunately, my father saved me by appearing at my side. I saw Elisande's eyes rake over his body – if he was embarrassed by her frank appraisal he gave no sign. I doubt he even noticed, however – he's comfortable in his own skin.

"You owe me a desk, Lady Elisande," he opened. "But welcome all to Purgatory. To The Inferno. My house is yours."

He directed them to a booth, gesturing to Ricky and Shiloh to bring refreshment. He winced slightly as his 'accessory' landed awkwardly on his shoulder, drawing blood.

"Do you have a name for him yet?" enquired Elisande, settling herself.

"Not formally – I gather he will let me know in his own time. I think of him as 'George'."

"George . . . the dragon." The Lady of the Blessed Isle, Queen of the Sidhe, laughed softly. "I was informed of your – sense of humour."

"That I have one?"

"That it can be – ah – weird," she replied deadpan, looking at me. I thought it might be a good time to assist with the music again. The look on my father's face seemed to agree.

"Ah – excuse me," I mumbled, bearing a hasty retreat.

"Will The Fallen be playing tonight?"

"We would be MOST disappointed if they did not – especially after Gethin has told us so much –"

I did not look at Gethin – I could hardly blame him. After all, we WERE hot! However, the mind boggled at how we were going to fit on stage in costume – and the possible political repercussions of refusal. The Sidhe Court had never come to my Domain before (and I had only recently been a guest in theirs for the first time) – and I was bound to ask 'why now?' The implications were, however, more than I chose to contemplate at this moment in time. Politics could take a backseat, at least temporarily.

My gaze flickered to Gethin's, but it was unreadable. He was keeping his own council. I had little choice but to sketch a graceful bow. "Then far be it for us to disappoint an audience." I was grateful to Ricky and Shiloh for a timely appearance at my elbow. "Be refreshed while we – ah – dress more appropriately." I half-bowed and hastily retreated to prep the guys. A frantic backstage costume change ensued.

"May the Force be with you," Mike said, almost tripping over his Jedi costume. "What's the playing order?"

"Let's just fly," I said, and I saw them look at each other. I meant that we would not play any set theme, any set order. Just let our instincts guide us. It was dangerous – usually we sensed what the audience wanted to hear and played. And played. And played our hearts out, on such wild nights. Perhaps I could persuade Gethin to join us on stage – Sidhe harps and fiddles were not usually heard outside their borders, but once heard they were never forgotten. It was the least he could do for dropping me in this mess, I thought. There would be little we could do which would shock our guests, I thought . . . and it might even help. I didn't usually let go of my barriers – but at the back of my mind was a driving need to cleanse myself.

Because soon, I was going to kill my mother.

"Let's go, guys!"

[There was a wild look in Luc's eyes, a look I hadn't seen for some time. Almost desperation. "Hold onto your nuts, guys, it's going to be a bumpy night," I murmured to Gabe, Peter and Paul as we preceded him out onto stage and took up our places. I was trying to second-guess where he was going, but wasn't really sure I wanted to. I knew Dam

was here somewhere, but there was no chance to talk to my real boss. Which caused me to question, when it came to the wall, who my REAL boss actually was. If I had to say, I knew I would say Lucifer, Prince of Darkness . . . and knew that it was time that a special force was formed, a special police force, if you like, independent of both Domains. I wondered if that was where Luc was trying to send me. I rather thought it was . . . but then, as he stepped onto stage and the room exploded, I forgot everything but keeping up with him. We all did. Luc led us – on stage and off . . . it was time we admitted it.

"Unchained," he said, his hair flying as his body took up the rhythm. He'd picked one hell of an opening number. It made your fingers bleed, if you let the music touch your soul. He could do that. Do it very well. Draw you in, draw you down, draw you on. Sense what his audience wanted to hear, wanted to feel – and take them wherever they wanted to go.

That's why he's so dangerous – and so good on stage.

And probably why he doesn't know it. Because it's deep within him, a part which lies hidden until he's out there performing his heart out. Few people know the battles Luc has fought to be where and what he is . . . rather than what people often expect him to be when they come to him or pray to him. I've been there with him through most of it. Hunted him and hunted for him . . . perhaps one day, ALL the details will become known . . . not just the version people think they know – or even the version HE tells. From the point of view of the others involved – namely The Fallen.

. . . But for now, all we could do is follow him, as always, on his wild ride.

And hang on for dear life!]

Having little to do beyond checking sound levels now that The Fallen were on stage, I took the opportunity to slip behind the bar. "How goes it?" I enquired, rolling up my sleeves and washing glasses.

"Well enough. They can certainly drink!"

I laughed. "Ask Gethin for a recipe or two – believe me, you haven't tasted anything like the stuff they brew!"

"I thought there was something about not drinking or eating in faerie," Ricky mused, frowning, as he passed me more glasses.

"An old wives' tale. I think," I added. "Is she holding up?"

"'She's doing just fine!" Shiloh responded, grinning cheekily at me. "'He' might not be, if the looks on some of her Court's faces is ought to go by!"

"That's why 'he' is over here doing the washing up," I retorted dryly. We DO have dishwashers – it just looks more – human, I suppose – to do it by hand. It can also be quicker.

"When do you suppose he will tell me my fate?" she blurted out, and at Ricky's affirmation I drew her to one side.

"How many times must I tell you not to worry? That you are free to do as you wish?" I asked her, gently touching her cheek with a damp hand.

"I know. I am foolish, I know – but I still wish to hear it from him."

I sighed, taking her hands in mine. "He will speak with you as soon as he is able, I know it. He HAS been rather – tied up – of late."

"I know who would LIKE to tie him up," murmured Shiloh, laughing softly as she looked across the room.

"Who are we tying up?" enquired Ashe, perching with difficulty on a stool.

"Shiloh was suggesting that our honoured guest would like to tie up a certain front man," I replied.

Ashe chuckled. "It could be fun. He might even enjoy it." Her eyes met mine and she winked. "It's one of the few occasions he doesn't have to be in control."

"There's control and control," I shrugged, glancing over her shoulder as Gethin approached. "Is he into bondage?"

"Who?"

"Father." I grinned at his puzzlement. "You know – tying up . . .?"

He probably picked up an image from my mind – I'll swear his cheeks coloured slightly. It could have been the lighting, I suppose.

"That's for him to tell, impudent child," he retorted, grinning. "I have been asked if you know where his fiddle is."

I gaped. I have always heard that one thing he never does is play his fiddle – his golden fiddle – in public. This probably meant that Gethin would play too. The only inference that came to mind was that something was going to happen which he did not wish to be remembered. Or perhaps it was simply the visit of the Sidhe to Purgatory. That, I thought, was probably cause enough.

Perhaps there would be a private party upstairs in the family apartments while below others slept. I saw Gethin's head dip fractionally.

"I'll get it," I promised, wiping my hands.

A short time later, I placed the case almost reverently in his hands. He smiled at me and thanked me, his eyes lingering on mine for a *moment as if searching to see if I understood what he was about to do. I did. I thought I did, at least. Lucifer's golden fiddle was special. Very special. Depending on how and what he played, he could take souls, or cause a dreamlike state of forgetfulness. A very old, very special magic that he used very rarely. Temptation, perhaps . . . or proof should I need it that he was not careless with power.*

I stepped to one side as he began to play, allowing the harmonics to wash over me. Those 'invited' moved up the long staircase almost in slow motion, as if moving through some dense medium. Behind the doors of his apartments, my father removed his costume in favour of a Sidhe-type loose robe before taking up his instrument again. I knew that this time, the music would be different. Was I prepared for this, I asked myself? There is no force, no – persuasion – beyond what lies within . . . and that is perhaps its danger. It lays bare what one most desires, deep in the recesses of one's mind – and it is not always pleasant to see what lies within. You have to be prepared for the consequences.

"Are you sure you want to stay?" I asked Shiloh. Part of me wanted her to stay desperately – wanted HER. Part of me did know what exposing her to this night might mean. Yet, as I looked from her to the place where my father and Gethin sat side by side, I could only wonder if there could be any harm.

"They're beautiful," she whispered, very softly. Did she mean the Sidhe, or my father and Gethin? Both were true.

Couples and groups separated from the mass in that same seeming slow motion as they played. I took her hand.

In truth, I remember little but waking next morning in Shiloh's arms and amidst a curtain of her hair. I dressed as quickly and quietly as I could.

"In such a hurry to depart?" asked a lazy voice from the tumbled bed.

"I did not want to wake you." My belly rumbled and I grinned apologetically. "See what I mean?"

"I rather think I do. I'll join you." She sprang from the bed, reaching for her clothes, unconcerned.

The kitchen was already well occupied by Mike and my father, who were cooking. Mike was wearing only a pair of dark combats, a cloth tucked in the waistband. For a soldier of long standing, he had few scars, I thought . . . which probably signified how good he really was. His hair was wild and uncombed – rather like Father's I thought. Only my father's hair was almost to the bottom of his ribcage, and really ought to be tied back if he was cooking. I was about to remark

on it (he was always going on about safety in the kitchen), when he
spun around to greet us and I caught a glimpse of the tattoo that now
graced his back by way of the mirror behind him as his hair swirled.
Impressive.

"Ah, more mouths to feed." He smiled a greeting. I caught a glimpse
of scratch marks (not all dragon-talons!), and thought I saw a strap-
burn at his wrist, but thought it wiser not to comment. "What can we
do you for?"

"What's cooking?" I asked, joining them at the griddle.

"Whatever your heart desires," Mike chuckled. "If we've got it and
'George' hasn't eaten it."

"Or The King."

"Or The King," Mike echoed. My eyes travelled into the corner,
where Elvis and 'George' were happily devouring – something.

"Just dish it up," I said. "You don't need to tell us what it is." I
pulled up a stool next to Shiloh, and we sat there with our cutlery
poised in expectation. "Have our guests departed?"

"Long ago." Father replied. "Gethin escorted them home – he should
be back soon." He seated himself, finally, a mug of coffee in his hands.
"I hear you are still concerned for your future, my child," he said so
suddenly that Shiloh started, taken aback. I knew she had expected an
'interview', but hardly in the kitchen!

"Yes – my Lord."

His eyes rolled and his lips twitched. "I think you ought to call
me Luc, at least, don't you? In the circumstances?" He did not name
the circumstances. Did not say whether he referred to her as my lover,
or the fact that he was perched on a kitchen stool, barefoot and bare-
chested, looking as dishevelled as if he had been dragged through a hedge
backwards, so to speak. How could he look such a mess, in a manner
of speaking, and still look as sexy as – hell – I wondered, catching the
flicker of a smile. "Just a gift, I guess," he murmured for my ears alone,
flicking his eyes to one side, indicating that I should help Mike load the
dishwasher. I obeyed.

"Luc, then," she tried to smile. "Yes, I am still concerned."

"Do you want it in writing? Is my word not enough? What must
I do to convince you? Don't be afraid. I will say it this last time: You
may stay here as long as you wish – or move on. If you wish to move
on, we will ease your passage as well as we may. If hearing it from my
lips makes it more believable than from my son's, be it so spoken."

"Thank you," she said softly, at last convinced that we were telling
her the truth. Slipping to her feet and crossing to him, she planted a

*kiss on his cheek. "You need a shave, my Lord," she offered cheekily as
she passed.*

"Are you offering?" he enquired, meeting her gaze frankly.

*"Oh, I'm sure you have an abundance of volunteers," she responded,
more confidently. "We use a knife, you know." She winked at me as she
stood behind him.*

*He tilted his head back, baring his throat. "I know." Her hands were
on his face, and his held them in place. I recognised that look in his eyes
– heavy lidded, languorous; in any one else, I might have been jealous . .
. but I knew well what he was doing. If she was going to share my life,
she would share his in a sense of the word – and she needed to be easy
in his presence. It did not mean that she would be given any special
privileges because she shared my bed . . . any more than he would go
easy on anyone who shared HIS . . . but his sense of humour could
be rather extreme at times – as could some of the other things, which
went on. She needed to be at ease with all of us – and it had to start
somewhere.*

*"I'll go give them a hand downstairs," she laughed, pulling her
hands free. He did not prevent her – one step at a time.*

*"I think I'll help," I said, leaving my father and Mike to sort out
the kitchen. With a bit of luck, they would have already sorted things
out downstairs and we could go for a ride. I was itching to try out my
new toy.*

"So – when are you going to The Tower?"

"So anxious, Michael?" I returned.

"I want it over," he shrugged. "I want peace – and there will
always be a threat as long as she lives. Do you want company?"

"Why you?"

He shrugged. "You won't ask Dam – someone should represent
him. You shield him too much."

Did I? Perhaps. Older brother's privilege.

"Ah well. Come, if you wish. I confess, I'd be glad of the
company."

He nodded once. "Alright then."

*[He wasn't as blasé about Gaia as he appeared to be, I knew . . . he
was not hard to read, even were I not practised at reading men. He had
banished her once, I knew he could banish her further, deeper if he chose
– but he knew I was right. She would find a way to come back. She had
proved her ability to do so well enough. Yet, I understood why he was*

reluctant, even if he would not admit to reluctance. I could offer to do it in his place, so that the blood was not on his hands, so to speak – but I did not. Why? Because I knew that if I voiced the thought, he would protest that the responsibility was his – that the threat was against him – that the right was his. All true . . . but he was still her son. They were still her sons, he and Dam. Slayer was his weapon. I knew all that. I knew all that and more. Which was why I was going with him, not just representing Dam, or as Luc's friend. Not even 'family'. I was going with him because I MUST.]

I was glad I had Mike at my side, in truth, as we made that journey. Déjà vu was strong as I drew my Hummer to a halt at the foot of The Tower. I was dressed as I had been before, in my long white coat, and I had Slayer loose in my hand. Together, we climbed the long staircase, each step seeming to take forever.

I knew all the reasons for my presence, but it did not make any step easier than the last.

I knew the consequences, both personal and public, which were going to echo through the realms.

I knew it all – but still I faltered at the doorway, reluctant to open it.

It was Mike's hand that keyed the opening. Mike who stepped through the doorway first.

Mike, who placed his hand over mine on Slayer's hilt.

She rose as we entered, something akin to acceptance on her face. She opened her lips as if to speak, but whether in a plea for forgiveness or in defiance, I will never know.

I felt my hand tense on Slayer, as the blade was raised.

I saw the smile on Michael's lips, felt his hand move on mine.

"MICHAEL!!!!!!!! . . . "

ENDGAME.

CHECKMATE

The End . . .?

A Soldier's Tale

Someone once said that time is like a river, and that our kind dip our toes into it from time to time without really taking the plunge. That is to say without getting involved. That might be true, for some. For others, it might be akin to a phobia. A fear of getting *too* involved.

Shall I tell you, perhaps, what really happened on that day long passed?

Are you just a little bit curious?

Perhaps you prefer the version you have grown used to. The 'official' version.

Perhaps you prefer the version HE tells. Luc, I mean. Lucifer. Lucifero diAngelus, child of angels. Firstborn.

Oh, that part's true enough. It's also true that Jayce was always Gaia's favourite. Why? Perhaps because he looked less like his father and more like her. Perhaps because he was more likely to say 'yes' than 'no' to her schemes. Luc was always – perverse. And likely to say 'no' just to annoy her.

Matthias had just left her. Not for the first time, true, but this time it looked likely to be permanent. (She always told the story that she had thrown him out – but few believed it privately. Publicly – well, do I need to spell it out?) Gaia was always a cold, calculating, power-hungry bitch. If I'd been Matthias, I'd have left long before.

We grew up together, Jayce, Luc and me, Michael – Dam following a few years later. Gabe, Peter and Paul – we were the core. The Inner Circle.

Jayce never had the following that Luc had. Oh, he had his circle of friends, but even he hovered around his more charismatic brother . . . and was content that it be so. Do not doubt that – they loved each other. Luc knew that Jayce did not want the throne – but he also knew that his twin did not have the strength to refuse their powerful mother. If Luc made any mistake, it was doubting his brother's inner strength when it came to taking the only way out he could see rather than betray his brother.

Was Luc plotting to overthrow his mother? Of course not! Luc never wanted the Upper Domain. He's telling the truth there. Better to rule in Hell than serve in Heaven – right? Because to rule in Heaven meant to rule in her name, and he would never be happy doing that.

What he DID plan was to go his own way. He only ever wanted Purgatory. He never really 'wanted' the Lower Domain – Hell. He just wanted to be left alone.

Gaia would not believe that. She took any refusal to do what she wanted as rebellion. She told Luc to come to her apartments on that fateful day, but Luc had other plans.

Do you want to know what really went down? If so, read on. If not, might I suggest you pour yourself a drink, put on the TV – whatever turns you on. Goodbye. Farewell. Adieu. Ciao. Au revoir. Auf wiedersehen.

Still reading? Good.

To explain properly, I need to retrace my steps a little. Explain a little better, perhaps, the people we were.

We were Gaia's golden boys, in those days: Gabe, Pete, Paul, Matthew, Mark, Luke, John and I. Her honour guard, to all intents: her private army. We used to hang out in Purgatory, at a dive called the Black Cauldron.

Purgatory was different then to now. It was a pretty lawless place, to tell you the truth. Blood and sawdust, if you catch my drift. Roughnecks, soldiers, wastrels. And Luc.

The Fallen started life in those days, but we weren't called that then. I don't recall what we were called – it'll no doubt come to me. Something 'clever' and 'arty', I suppose.

Jayce never played – he wasn't musical. He just – well – hovered, I suppose. Luc would sing, when he'd drunk enough, or smoked something that smelled truly foul . . . I think the snake came from one of those heavy nights. I still remember him walking in that night: stripped to the waist, black leather trousers, jacket carried loosely over his shoulder, his hair lank and loose, several days' growth on his face. He looked like he'd really tied one on. Then I saw the tattoo – that beautiful snake – met his eyes. Saw the defiance and laughter there. He knew it'd piss Gaia off royally. I could even hear her: "How dare you mar your beautiful body . . ."

I heard Jayce chuckle, "Nice one, bro."

"I thought so," he responded, tossing his jacket over a chair. "Shall we play?"

I didn't like his mood that night, I recall. Bitter, almost. Savage. Jayce, I could see, didn't like it either. "Luc has been having words with Mother," he whispered to me, later.

I was concerned enough to approach Gaia. In hindsight, not the wisest thing I have ever done.

"I do not think it is any of your business, Michael."

"On the contrary, if it concerns security, it concerns me greatly," I reasoned.

"I had a disagreement with my son – is that so unusual?" She smiled. She was trying to appear – well, the only description that comes to mind is like a normal mother. Gaia was never that. Never. Not even, I gather, the day they were born. I'm told that she handed them over to Matthias and a nurse and went straight back to work. I wasn't there at the time, but it would run true to form.

"I have a wilful son. He enjoys – winding me up. Is that the right term?" I nodded. "I offered him a job – he refused. I shall offer it to Jason instead." It was then she told me of her plans to step down. I didn't believe her any more than Luc had. But I never believed she'd let him leave, either.

Why did he want to leave? It was his time, you might say – but to stay meant losing his freedom, being her mouthpiece. He was not overtly political, which was why he wanted Purgatory. Purgatory is neutral territory. A non-interference zone. He never actually wanted Hell as well. He sort of fell into that one . . . but I get ahead of myself. I made the mistake of agreeing with Luc when he voiced his opinions of his mother's real motives. And Jayce made the mistake of doubting Luc's anger at her interference.

Where was Dam during all this? Being younger, he wasn't supposed to frequent 'The Cauldron' . . . but sometimes he'd sneak in. (We've all done it, right?) He heard what was said, and the venom in Luc's voice. Much of it was alcohol fired, true – much of it hot air – but Dam didn't know that. So when Gaia found out he'd been there and asked him what had been said – told him that no one would be hurt, that there'd be no reprisals – well, he told the truth as he knew it. What he'd heard –

And saw the horror on Jayce's face. I told Jayce to find Luc and warn him. To give him time to get out, if he could . . . but I should have known Luc would not run.

I should have known he would walk right into her office and face her down. Tell her to get the hell out of his life and leave him alone.

She told him he was just like his father – but in language which made even me blush. We held him from her, Jayce and I. He could have killed her then and there, I think, had we not. It might, in retrospect, have been better for us all if he had.

She swore to teach him a lesson – one he would never forget . . . and so she did, but not perhaps the one she intended.

She taught us ALL a lesson – about the misuse of power.

There was chaos for a while . . . I tried to comfort Dam and stop Jayce from doing something he would regret. I did not see them take Luc; I would have prevented it if I had, whatever the consequences. By the time I found out, her hired dogs had him deep in The Mansion's dungeons. By the time we found him, Gabe and I, they had him bound on the rack. Their instructions had been to 'get rid of that damned snake'. I leave it to your imagination HOW. A mother's love, right?

I held them at bay while Gabe took him down. We helped him out of the dungeon, and Rafe and Phoenix opened doors for us that she had ordered closed. If it cost us our jobs, we did not care. So, when Luc says I escorted him out of Heaven, he's telling the truth, sort of. But I did not 'kick him out', as the popular version would have it. Why didn't I go with him? Even to this day, I'm not sure. Perhaps because he'd asked me to stay and look after Dam – and Jayce. Perhaps because he'd asked me to intercede between her and our people. Perhaps because he'd ask me to look after Phoenix. (Gaia hadn't liked that little aspect. She hadn't liked it at all. Phoenix was one of her favourites – and when she found out Phoenix was sneaking into Purgatory with a certain person who was not exactly in favour . . . not when she had a 'nice boy' chosen out for her favourite . . . someone who might not be interested in 'soiled goods', so to speak . . .) Choose your reason – it might be the right one. Or not.

I failed with Jayce. I really screwed up there. Jayce didn't want to take Luc's place. I know he argued with Gaia. Asked her to forgive Luc. To wait. To be patient.

Gaia is not patient by nature. She pushed Jayce – and for once, Jayce defied her. He walked out. Told her to cool it. Decided to go on an 'operation' to chill out – and got in over his head. Gaia, of course, milked it for all it was worth. Played the martyr angle – and made sure Luc got word. Let him know that Jayce was in deep shit . . . let him know the price of Jayce's 'salvation' – his surrender – and made sure Jayce knew it too. That his survival was dependent on his twin's surrender.

The bravest thing Jayce ever did was take himself out of the equation.

It changed nothing – and everything.

Even at the end, I think he hoped that his mother would step in, would find some spark of love, some gem of decency and send help. I wonder how it felt as he realised she had rejected him as tainted, useless, just as she had Luc. That her eyes were already looking elsewhere.

I even contemplated joining those who chose to depart, despite the promises I had made to Luc. Somehow, we had persuaded her to let 'the rebels' leave, if they wanted. That it was better to have them out of our hair than under our heels. I'm not sure how we did it. I hope it was a spark of humanity, but I doubt it. She probably intended to use it from the start as a 'rallying call'. To brainwash those who stayed behind, and humanity in general that she was the wronged one . . . that Luc was the evil one. I guess it worked, sort of. Perhaps Luc should have made some attempt at counter-propaganda . . . but as I said, he wasn't a political animal, not then. He learned, over the years, and learned well . . . but he plays by his rules.

As I watched them leave, my friends many of them, sent them onward in her name, I truly wanted to join them. But I had given my word, and I was not going to break it like she had. However much it hurt. Which is why I seem to spend more time downstairs than up, particularly these days. Mind you, Gaia always thought it was her idea to have me spy on him. An eye in the enemy camp, right? Which I did, with Luc's full knowledge and cooperation. Disinformation, you might say. In case you wondered.

So, there you have it. Short and sweet. The Fall.

How did Luc end up with both Hell AND Purgatory?

That, as they say, is another story.

Still here?
Hungry for more?

You want to know how he actually ended up with the Lower Domain, right? Hell.

It's actually quite simple, and a sort of accident, really.

It wasn't easy, getting Purgatory organised. It really was a frontier town in those days . . . but Luc was nothing if not organised. He wanted this. Wanted it bad. Wanted to succeed so that he could prove to his mother that he was every bit as good as she was. Better. Different, but better. So, he gathered people to him. Spike and Jude go way back with him, got things started along with a few others. A few broken bones, a few twisted arms . . . that sort of thing. Law and order.

Soon, Ricky turned up on his doorstep, and walked into the fledgling INFERNO, saying he was the best barman and manager there had ever been, and he might be willing to allow them to employ him. Luc had liked him straight away, and set him to organising. It was Ricky who had hired the 'Angels', generally hiring and firing with Luc's passive approval. If he disapproved, he spoke out. If not, Ricky carried on as he pleased. It was that sort of arrangement, and it worked.

Hell, in those days, was run by a guy by the name of Stan. Yeah. Stan. He wasn't too happy with Luc's presence in Purgatory, thought it smacked of nepotism (he had somehow managed to miss out on the fact that not only did Gaia not want Luc in Purgatory, she would have been perfectly happy if he had ceased to exist at all!). He had sent his heavies in to, well, sort Luc out. Luc had sent them back. In pieces. Or should I say pizzas? Yeah, you got it. In pizza delivery boxes.

Well, Spike and Jude did. Luc didn't know about it until afterwards, when Stan turned up on his doorstep demanding retribution.

I ought to point out that Stan wasn't exactly liked . . . and that more than a few people who frequented The Inferno had dropped hints that they would rather like him out of the way. Luc, however, was content to 'live and let live' – until Stan started throwing his weight about.

All sound and thunder, etc.

Luc had stood looking at him, trying very hard not to laugh in his face, before turning his back and simply walking away. Stan had taken exception to this, and raised his weapon with intent to strike. I still say that Slayer had leapt into Luc's hand, rather than Luc physically drawing it, but he turned, and the blade went right into Stan of its own volition. Simple. End of play.

However, according to their rules, if Luc took him out, he automatically got the job. He protested, of course – offered to find them someone else, but they'd seen what he'd done for Purgatory, made it 'respectable', and wanted the same for themselves. Fair, right? So he agreed to stay – to get the place in order, staff and all, and then when they were ready, he'd have full and proper elections.

I guess they're not ready yet, because he's still there, and somewhat resigned to it.

So, there you have it. My version of what happened . . . or as much as I'm prepared to tell. A guy has to have his secrets, right? So, until next time, it's goodbye from me, and goodbye from him . . .